Praise

'Prabhu Dayal's novella, The Surajpur Connection, is written with verve and spirit, that takes the reader though an effortless but engaging journey into the heart of India, and the mystery that surrounds the life of a kidnapped child. It is also a serious indictment of the issue of child kidnapping, and the syndicate that operates it. I thoroughly enjoyed reading the book.'

Pavan Varma
Former M.P. and Author

'I have always known my childhood friend Prabhu Dayal to be a gifted writer. In his book' The Surajpur Connection', he draws on some of his experiences from the Gulf Arab countries where he has served for many years and offers the reader an unputdownable masterpiece. Written in an elegant style, it is recommended reading for young and old alike'.

Vivek Katju
Former Ambassador and Secretary, Ministry of External Affairs

'Ambassador Prabhu Dayal is an accomplished diplomat and a master story teller. "The Surajpur Connection", is a gripping trans-cultural and trans-national tale of a boy born into a family of wealthy landlords. Grappling with some troublesome and traumatising issues, it takes you to the heartland of India; it is a thriller that engages the reader while also asking some deeper questions. Strongly recommended, the book promises to be a riveting read'.

Saurabh Shukla
Author, Founder and Editor in Chief
NewsMobile

In his new book 'The Surajpur Connection', Ambassador Prabhu Dayal, author of the best-selling book 'Karachi Halwa' weaves a tale of many strands, some happy, some sad. Many twists and turns await the reader, who is constantly intrigued by the question: Will the journey of the child across time and nations end in triumph or tragedy?

Niraj Srivastava
Former Ambassador

Also by Prabhu Dayal

Karachi Halwa

THE SURAJPUR CONNECTION

Prabhu Dayal

Illustrations by Chandini Dayal

ZORBA BOOKS

ZORBA BOOKS

Published in India by Zorba Books, 2018

Website: www.zorbabooks.com
Email: info@zorbabooks.com

Copyright © Prabhu Dayal
Illustrations by Chandini Dayal

ISBN Print Book - 978-93-87456-21-1
ISBN eBook - 978-93-87456-22-8

Zorba Books Pvt. Ltd.(opc)
Gurgaon, INDIA

Printed at Repro Knowledgecast Limited, Thane

Dedicated to

PRAYAS
and its founder
Amod Kanth
an international 'model of public service'
on behalf of India's children

Disclaimer

Part One

He knew immediately that the clue which he needed had arrived.

He had been sitting on the sofa in his suite in the Taj Mahal Hotel in Mumbai, reading 'India Times', when a report in the paper caught his attention.

He read the report with a sense of disbelief. He had not expected to stumble upon such information, and he could hardly control his excitement.

He put down the newspaper and thought for a few moments; no doubt, all his plans for the next few days would have to be altered.

A little while later, he rang up his wife. "Darling, I will not be returning tonight. Something unexpected has come up, and I will have to stay in India for a few more days. Please have the Board meeting postponed".

"What is more important than the Board meeting? You had yourself asked for it to be convened for deciding the road map for the next five years", she said, adding, "The others will be upset at a last-minute cancellation".

"Something very important has cropped up, but I can't say anything more right now", he replied. "I will not be in Mumbai during the next few days, though I can be reached on my cell phone.".

She tried to persuade him again: "You can always go back next week after the Board meeting".

However, his mind was already made up. "Please do as I say and have the meeting postponed. You can offer the excuse that I have fallen ill and hence my return will be delayed by a few days. Also, please tell everyone that I should not be disturbed—doctor's orders or something like that".

There was an inflexibility in his tone which she had rarely noticed before. She was understandably curious. What was holding him back in India? Why was he not giving her some idea?

Is there some woman out there, she wondered? However, she dismissed the thought, for he was not the sort of person who was given to chasing skirts or saris; work was his all-consuming passion.

"All right" she said somewhat reluctantly, "I will do as you want, dear".

"Love you, bye", he said as he hung up.

Deep in thought, he gazed out of the window. The Arabian Sea stretched as far as the eye could see, with the luscious waves buffeting the coast.

His mind was also being buffeted by a multitude of thoughts. He examined his options; how should he proceed?

He did not want to waste any time-- that was for sure. So, he called up his travel agent and made some enquiries. The travel agent gave him the information he wanted.

"In that case, please book my tickets for the flight as well as for the train".

"I will have to check the availability, sir".

"All right, do that. But let me know as soon as possible".

The travel agent called back within an hour to convey that his bookings had been made on the flight leaving for Delhi at 3 pm as well as for the onward train journey from there. A limousine had also been arranged in Delhi to take him from the airport to the railway station.

It was almost noon when, he checked out of the Taj Mahal Hotel and headed for the airport. The flight was on time.

His heart was beating faster than it had ever done before, and he could hardly control his excitement.

✦ ✦ ✦

To the manor born

1

The 1967 General Elections were going to be held throughout India after a few months, and they had already captured public fancy as nothing else had done since the country's independence two decades earlier. Nehru's daughter Indira Gandhi was now the leader of the Congress party, and political analysts were wondering whether she would be able to garner as much support from voters as her illustrious father had done.

A tall, well-built and handsome man, Ram Singh Chaudhary took a keen interest in politics, though he had turned down offers from several political parties to be their candidate for the State Assembly from Handia, a constituency located in the eastern part of Allahabad where Chandrapur, his village was situated.

The phone rang, and Ram Singh got up from his chair.

"Hello", he said in his usual calm and composed manner.

"Namaskar, Ram Singh *ji*. This is Rajendra Gupta calling. I am sorry if I have been troubling you so much during the past few days. The party High Command is insisting that I speak to you once more and request you to change your mind". Gupta, the General Secretary of the Congress Party in Uttar Pradesh, had been trying to persuade Ram Singh to be their candidate in the coming elections.

Ram Singh did not think for even a moment before replying: "Gupta *ji*, I am honoured that the Congress Party and you yourself think that I am worthy of being your candidate, but I am a bit preoccupied with my personal matters, and therefore I will not have the time to contest the elections. Please forgive me".

It was only natural for political parties to court Ram Singh. For several generations, his family of '*zamindars*'(land-owners) had been pre-eminent not just in Chandrapur but in this entire agricultural belt which lay on the eastern part of Allahabad district. He and his younger brother Shyam Singh Chaudhary jointly owned the family's vast estate, and their families lived together in the imposing mansion which had stood there for over fifty years.

Secretly, most parties hoped that if he contested as their candidate, he would fund not only his own election campaign but also donate generously to the party's coffers. After all, money is mother's milk for elections.

However, Ram Singh had no desire to be a candidate in these elections. Firstly, he did not want to be seen going around from place to place asking for votes; he was too shy to do any such thing. Secondly, he did not want to risk defeat and humiliation, as he felt that one could never be sure of the outcome in an election; what if the goodwill which he enjoyed did not get translated into electoral votes? Above all, his life had suddenly been filled with joy as he had been blessed with a son, and he did not want to get distracted by the rough and tumble of political life.

While Ram Singh was not prepared to enter the political fray himself, he hoped that one day his new-born son would do so. He wanted the infant to become not just rich but famous too when he grew up. "He will be the Prime Minister of India one day", he often boasted to his wife.

❑ ❑ ❑

Ram Singh stood in the verandah and looked at his farm; it stretched as far as he could see. The landscape was green and yellow, resplendent with the ripening mustard crop.

In just a few weeks, the landscape would change. The fields would be harvested, summer would set in and the earth would be completely brown and parched; not even a blade of grass would be seen anywhere on these fields. Hot winds would blow dust in one's face; the village folk would finish their chores in the morning and then venture out as little as possible in the afternoons, whiling away their time indoors as best as they could. Summer would be so different from spring.

Ram Singh often wondered why was everything so transitory, and why the ephemeral was the only eternal?

Though she had been married to him for fifteen years, Devika, had remained childless. Then, four months back she had given birth to a beautiful boy. It was as if the long, frigid winter had given way to spring; his despair had been replaced by happiness and fulfilment.

What if such happiness were to be snatched away from him and replaced by sadness, just as bountiful spring gives way to the harshness of an Indian summer?

Ram Singh brushed aside such unpleasant thoughts and went inside the house. He wanted to see what his infant son was doing. The little baby meant more to him than anything else in the world.

His son was asleep; he gently caressed his cheek. Then, he left the house for a round of his farm to see how things were going on out there.

❑ ❑ ❑

Ram Singh had named the new born 'Shiva' after the Hindu deity whose blessings had no doubt been vital for ending the drought in his life. He had tried everything possible in his quest for an heir. He had consulted numerous physicians and consumed considerable doses of traditional as well as modern medicine. He and Devika had gone on pilgrimages to countless shrines and holy places, but to no avail. Finally, as advised by the family astrologer, he had built a temple of Lord Shiva in the village.

Shiva is regarded by Hindus as Mahadeva (or the Great God) and has many forms, both benevolent as well as fearsome. At the highest level, Shiva is transcendent, limitless, unchanging and formless. In benevolent aspects he is depicted as an omniscient yogi who lives an ascetic life on Mount Kailash in the Himalayas, as well as a householder who lives with his wife Parvati and his two children Ganesh and Kartikeya. In fierce aspects, he is often depicted as slaying demons.

In the temple which he had built, Ram Singh installed a ten-foot high statue of Shiva having all the usual iconographic aspects --the third eye on his forehead, the snake around his neck, his matted hair adorned by a crescent and with the river Ganga flowing from it, the 'trishul' or trident as his weapon and the 'damru' or two-headed drum.

In the courtyard of the temple, there was a black granite 'Shiva Linga' or genital organ of Lord Shiva. The 'Shiva Linga' is worshipped by Hindus as a symbol of the generative power of the deity; they believe that there is a mysterious 'Shakti' or power in the 'Shiva Linga'.

Thus, when Ram Singh's wife gave birth to a son after fifteen years of marriage, he was sure that Lord Shiva had answered his prayers. He had vowed, "I will go to the temple every day to thank Lord Shiva".

The women of the village, however would say to one another in hushed voices that last winter Devika had spent a month in her village to look after her aged mother, and one did not know whom she met and what happened there; perhaps that was Lord Shiva's way of helping her.

Of course, the village women were quite incorrigible, and they just loved to gossip about everyone.

13

Maternity is a fact, but paternity is often only a belief. Ram Singh believed that he had been blessed with a son due to Lord Shiva's divine intervention, and that is what really mattered.

❏ ❏ ❏

To celebrate the birth of his son, Ram Singh threw a lavish party to which over a thousand guests were invited. The entire village of Chandrapur was lit up as if it was Deepawali, or the festival of lights. Music resonated all around, and colourfully attired village girls presented dances to felicitate Ram Singh and Devika for the birth of their son.

Ram Singh and Devika doted on the infant. As the days went by and he started to grow up, Ram Singh gave all sorts of toys to him. He loved to sit near his son and watch him play with these toys.

Devika wanted to keep the child in her lap all the time. He was a beautiful boy, and while Ram Singh had named the child 'Shiva', she preferred to call him by a pet name she gave him—Sonu, which means handsome.

Thus, Sonu became the name by which everyone referred to the baby; it sounded so appropriate! When Devika would nestle him in her arms to make him sleep, she would often say to herself, "One day he will grow up to be such a handsome lad, and I will find the most beautiful bride for him".

The years rolled by; the seasons followed each other as they are accustomed to do. Sonu was going to be four years old in a few months. His mother had not agreed to send him to the nearby nursery school as she considered it sub-standard. Besides, she did not want him to waste his time there in the company of children who were not from the same social class. She had asked her husband to arrange a private tutor for him; after studying at home for a few years, he would be sent to a boarding school in Allahabad.

Thus, Sonu was free to play at home almost all day. He was loved by one and all-- at least this is what his parents thought. They were planning a big party to celebrate his fifth birthday as they had done every year.

□ □ □

The truth was that not everyone had been happy when Sonu arrived in this world. Shyam Singh was not pleased at all that his elder brother now had a son; this was even more true of his wife Radha. Since Devika had not borne a child for fifteen years, they had presumed that she was barren and had thus fancied their son Rajendra Singh (or Raju as everyone called him) to be the sole heir of the family estate.

Sonu's birth had changed the scenario. As things now stood, Raju and Sonu would jointly inherit the estate, as Ram Singh and his brother had done.

The estate was indeed enormous, and even after the proposed land reforms were implemented by the Government, it would yield enough wealth for both the boys. However, for so long had Raju's parents coveted the entire estate for their son that they were not happy with the changed circumstances.

Ironically, Raju himself did not harbor any malice towards his little cousin. He would visit the family home during the holidays as he was studying at a boarding school in Allahabad. Whenever he came home, he would play a lot with his little cousin. Ram Singh and Devika would be very happy to see the two children together. However, this was not the case with Shyam Singh and Radha. However, they feigned utmost affection towards Sonu, and no one could really guess how much they disliked him.

❑ ❑ ❑

One day, Radha had an outburst when she was visiting her brother Vijay Bahadur Singh, a wealthy landowner who stayed in another village a few miles away from Chandrapur.

He had casually asked her, "When will Sonu start going to school".

Instead of answering his query, Radha shouted angrily, "Do I care? I hate Sonu, and I wish that he had never been born". She continued her rant: "If he had not been there, my son Raju would have been the sole heir of the estate.

I don't know how that witch Devika bore a child after not having done so for fifteen years".

She carried on speaking for almost ten minutes about her dislike for Sonu and his parents.

Although Vijay did not say anything to her, he was concerned that this matter was so badly disturbing his sister's equanimity and peace of mind. "Perhaps, I should do something to sort it out", he told himself.

During the next few weeks, Vijay began to visit his sister's house much more frequently than before. He brought small gifts for Sonu each time he came there—chocolates, candy, balloons, small toys and many other such trinkets which always make little children happy. He would also play childish games with Sonu and take him out for rides in his car.

As a result, the little boy became very fond of him and would run to him whenever he saw him coming. Ram Singh and Devika were happy that Vijay was so fond of their son. Radha, on the other hand was rather cross with her brother on this account, though she did not say anything to him.

□ □ □

It was just an average day in September 1970; it had rained for a few hours in the morning, and the air was humid and sultry. It was now past mid- day, and Ram Singh and Devika were resting in their bedroom after lunch; the breeze from the ceiling fan was making them rather sleepy. In any case, they liked taking a snooze every afternoon.

Devika had nestled Sonu in her arms and tried to put him to sleep by singing a lullaby. While she as well as her husband had soon dozed off, Sonu just lay quietly on the bed beside his mother.

Then, seeing his chance, he slipped out of the room to play downstairs, as he often did while his parents rested in the afternoon.

Vijay had come to visit his sister, and as he was leaving he saw Sonu playing by himself in the verandah. He also noticed that there was no one else around.

"Come with me, I have some chocolates for you in my car", Vijay whispered as he lifted Sonu in his arms.

Sonu was happy. "Uncle Vijay, you are so nice", he said.

No one saw Vijay holding Sonu in his arms as he paced towards the porch where his car was parked.

"Do you want to come for a ride in my car", he asked.

Sonu nodded, as he was fond of car rides.

Vijay opened the door, and Sonu excitedly clambered on to the back seat. Vijay gave him a chocolate bar.

No one saw them drive away from there.

When Devika woke up from her afternoon siesta, she began looking for Sonu, as it was time to give him a glass of milk. She gave him two big glasses every day; he liked fresh milk, though he fussed sometimes and wanted to have tea instead like his father did. She would tell him that milk was good for him, that if he drank milk everyday he would grow up to be strong like his father, and then he could drink as much tea as he wanted.

"Sonu, come here", she called out aloud, but he did not show up.

"Where are you, Sonu"?

She thought that he was hiding somewhere as he often did, so she looked for him in the next room, and then the next.

He was nowhere to be seen and therefore, she woke up Ram Singh.

The servants, who had by now returned from their afternoon rest also began to look for him everywhere in the house and then in the garden, but Sonu was not found anywhere.

Ram Singh told the servants to search the whole house more thoroughly, but their search was again fruitless.

Darkness had begun to fall, and Ram Singh decided to go to the police station and report that his son was missing. Perhaps they would be able to find him. Everyone realized the gravity of the situation. Ram Singh and Devika prayed that their child was safe, and that some tragedy had not befallen him.

+ + +

Snatched away

2

With Sonu sitting happily on the back seat of his car, Vijay had driven straight to his own house. The little boy had been there a few times with his cousin Raju.

Vijay lived there alone as he had not married. Since it was a hot afternoon, there were no servants hanging around as they were resting in their quarters.

He gave Sonu another bar of chocolate to make him feel happy. He also gave him a ball to play with.

Thus, having ensured that Sonu was happily occupied, Vijay made a telephone call.

A little while later, another car arrived at his house.

Vijay told Sonu, "Some urgent work has come up, and I am going to be busy. My friend will take you home".

He then took Sonu to the car which had just arrived and helped him get inside. He waved Sonu goodbye as the car drove away.

After about ten minutes, the car reached another house, and the driver asked Sonu to come with him. Sonu got out of the car, wondering where they had come, as this was not his house.

"I want to go home", he said.

"I will take you home soon", the driver of the car replied, and he took Sonu inside the house.

A burly, bearded man wearing a turban was seated on a sofa as they entered the house, and he asked Sonu to come near him.

"You are such a sweet little boy', he said to Sonu as he patted him on his cheek. "So sweet", he said again and again.

Then he turned to the man who had brought Sonu to this house. "He is just the right age", he remarked as he again patted the little boy on his cheek. He put Sonu on his lap and asked affectionately, "Do you want to have some water"? Since it was hot, Sonu was thirsty and he nodded. He was given a glass of water which he drank quickly.

Lifting Sonu in his arms, the turbaned man began to walk up and down the room, humming softly. Sonu felt happy and put his head on the man's shoulder. Soon, he was fast asleep; this was hardly surprising, as a sleeping tablet had been dissolved in the glass of water.

❑ ❑ ❑

No one had any idea about what had been brewing in Vijay's mind since Radha's outburst a few months ago; if this boy was a thorn in his sister's flesh, then he would just remove that thorn.

Radha was unaware of the criminal side of her brother's personality, for he kept it well concealed beneath a soft spoken and polished veneer. In his teens, he had raped and murdered a minor girl from his village who was the daughter of a poor labourer on his farm. The girl's body was never found as Vijay had thrown it into the river which flowed nearby, where it had been devoured by hungry crocodiles.

This aspect of his character had developed steadily; he had become more and more emboldened as the years passed and was now a hardened criminal. The people of this area did not have had any clue about the heinous crimes which he was involved in. However, this was the first time that he had struck at a target within his circle of close relatives.

In fact, Ram Singh's cook had told him: "I had seen Vijay *Saheb* come to the house earlier, just as I was going home to rest in the afternoon. Maybe Sonu went out with him".

Accordingly, Ram Singh had telephoned Vijay. "We cannot find Sonu in the house. Did he go with you when you left from here"?

Vijay had replied in the negative.

❑ ❑ ❑

The house where Sonu had been sent by Vijay belonged to Mahinder Singh, a middle-aged man who hailed from Delhi. He had come to this village only a few years back and had bought a small tract of farm land where he had employed just a few workers.

25

Mahinder had also constructed a house there. A high wall had been built around the house so separate it from the rest of the farm, for Mahinder wanted privacy.

Mahinder lived in his farmhouse most of the time but went sometimes to Delhi since his family resided there. His wife and children hardly ever visited him as they found village life to be very unattractive and dull as compared to the life in Delhi, which had glittering shopping arcades, cinema houses and restaurants. His cousin Joginder lived on the farm house with him, and served as his Man Friday-- driver, cook and house keeper. He was also in charge of running the farm.

It was Joginder who had driven the car which brought Sonu from Vijay's house. It was he who had dissolved the sleeping tablet in the glass of water which Mahinder had given to Sonu.

❑ ❑ ❑

In fact, Vijay and Mahinder were partners in running a child kidnapping racket. Vijay's men would pick up children from schools, homes, parks, market places and wherever else they could lay their hands on them. The blindfolded children would then be delivered to Mahinder, who would keep them in the basement of his farmhouse.

The kidnapped children would not know where they were being held; this was felt necessary if they were going to be returned after collecting ransom.

In some cases, however the ransom amount was too high and could not be paid by the parents; in some other cases, the children were from poor families and making a demand for ransom was unnecessary. Such children met a terrible fate: they would be sold off to traffickers and were never heard of again.

The traffickers would terrorize the kidnapped children by repeatedly thrashing and torturing them, for example by burning their faces, hands and feet with cigarette butts. In this manner, they would force the children into complete submission.

Sometimes, the abducted children were taken to some place in a totally different part of the country; a leg or a hand would be surgically cut off or they would be blinded in one or both eyes. Many such children died from the trauma. Those who survived were made to beg on the streets. The process of thrashing them mercilessly would continue until they became completely terrorized, obedient and submissive.

These children were sometimes so young that they did not even know where their parents lived. Fate had condemned them, and they were totally at the mercy of their captors.

Gangs like this one were operating all over the country. Thousands of such kidnappings took place every year, with most of the children just disappearing and never being found. People wondered whether some police officials were also involved, for how else could such kidnappings take place so frequently, and so brazenly at that?

In the case of Sonu, there was no question of asking for a ransom, as Vijay just wanted the boy out of the way. He chuckled with satisfaction over what he had just accomplished for his sister. He had ensured that her son would inherit the entire estate. He did not give a damn about what would happen to Sonu. If the boy survived the ordeal, he would perhaps lose a limb or two and then end up begging on the streets somewhere.

He had also decided that he would not tell his sister about what he had done. "Women can never keep secrets", he said to himself and sniggered.

❑ ❑ ❑

As luck would have it, Sonu was not going to lose his life or even a limb, for Mahinder had some other plan in mind. He had been approached by a contact to find boys who were around four to six years old as they were needed in some Arab country. Four hundred rupees would be paid for each boy, which was a tidy sum at that time.

Sonu fitted the bill as he was the right age. Still sedated, he was bundled off on the back seat of their car by Joginder and Maninder, who would take turns driving to Bombay. During the journey, they would give him more pills; anyone would think that the little boy was sleeping, as children often do during long journeys.

Luckily for them, there was no hold up of any sort; their car was not stopped at any police check post. This was not unusual, as police constables manning such check posts normally did not search private passenger cars; they generally carried out checks on trucks to see if any contraband goods were being carried by them.

They reached Bombay, handed over the sleeping child to a tall, bearded Arab named Hussain, collected four hundred rupees and then celebrated their successful mission over beer and *kababs*. After that, they checked into a modest hotel where they slept for the night before starting the return journey.

❑ ❑ ❑

When Sonu woke up, he did not know how long he had slept. He felt tired and drowsy, but he realized that he was in a strange environment.

He looked all around this place where he was now lying, and he felt scared. He saw that there were three other small boys lying near him. There were many sacks all around, like the ones on his father's farm which used to be filled with grain. It was very hot, and there was an unpleasant smell; he felt as if he was going to vomit.

Sonu could not understand where he was or what he was doing in such a place.

He wanted to go home to his parents; he felt guilty about leaving the house without telling them, for they would be worried about him.

He did not have any idea how much time had elapsed since he had left his house with Uncle Vijay. He began to cry out aloud out of anxiety and fear. A tall, bearded man came over and, in a very stern manner told him to be quiet. However, Sonu kept crying and saying that he wanted to go home.

"Take me home, take me home", he kept repeating.

The man shouted at him in a strange language. He also gave him a tight slap which stunned Sonu and silenced him momentarily. "This is what you will get if you ask me to take you home", he shouted at Sonu, which made him cry even more.

The commotion and noise woke up the other children, who also began to cry. The tall man gave all of them the same treatment as he had just meted out to Sonu. He hit each of them and told them to be quiet, and not to make any noise. However, they did not stop crying.

Then, he took them up the stairs, showed them the sea and threatened to throw them into it if they gave him any more trouble. Sonu had never seen the sea and was scared by its vast emptiness.

Being so young, Sonu could not comprehend why all this was happening, or where he was going. He was terrified, but he could not have ever imagined what untold miseries were in store for him as well as for these three other children.

❑ ❑ ❑

During the hours after Sonu's abduction, the police in Chandrapur combed the entire village in search of him, but without any success. Next morning, Ram Singh drove down to Allahabad and met the Superintendent of Police (or the S.P. as he was generally called) to apprise him about his son's disappearance and seek his help in finding him.

The S.P sent a telegraphic message to all the police stations in his jurisdiction to hunt for the boy's kidnappers, but they could not come up with any result. Next day, the S.P brought the matter to the attention of his boss, the Inspector General of Uttar Pradesh Police.

A state-wide search for locating Sonu was started by the Police authorities, but by then the kidnappers had already crossed into another state.

The Uttar Pradesh police could not find Sonu anywhere, and three days later, a nation-wide alert was launched for him. By then, Hussain's small cargo vessel carrying Sonu along with three other kidnapped boys was already on the high seas.

The ship....

3

As a matter of fact, a patrol boat of the Indian Coast Guard had routinely stopped the vessel while it was still in Indian territorial waters. The pilot of the patrol boat had come on board and asked Hussain if he was smuggling anything.

For a moment, Hussain had thought of teasing him and asking as to what was there to smuggle out of India, for gold, watches, textiles and electronic items were all smuggled into India, not out of it. However, he had refrained from saying any such thing for fear of annoying the officer; instead he had shown him the sacks of potatoes and rice that his small vessel was carrying. He had also offered him a packet of imported Dunhill cigarettes along with twenty rupees as 'a token of goodwill'.

The Coast Guard pilot had gone back to his patrol boat, quite happy that he had made some easy money. Not for a moment did he suspect that behind the sacks of rice and potatoes, there lay four small children who had been drugged and were being trafficked out of the country.

❑ ❑ ❑

The small ship, called a '*dhow*' in Arabic was heading towards the Persian Gulf. For centuries, Arab traders had used such ships to travel to India. They had carried pearls as well as dates, ivory and hides to Bombay, Malabar or Gujarat and brought back rice, sugar, spices onions, potatoes and whatever else was required not just by the people living in the small villages along the Persian Gulf coast but also in ports further away in Africa to where these Arab traders sailed every year.

Earlier, '*dhows*' had sails and used to be driven by wind power, but in recent times they had given way to more powerful vessels which had diesel engines, and which were much faster. This development had considerably shortened the travel time.

The cargo was carried below the deck in the hold of the vessel. This area had a lot of diesel fumes and was not suitable for human travel. However, this is where Sonu along with the three other children had been hidden.

The diesel fumes were making it difficult for the children to breathe. Moreover, the motion of the dhow as it made its way in the choppy waters of the Arabian Sea made Sonu feel very sick. He vomited, as did another child.

The children began to cry even louder than before. Hussain beat them once more, this time with a stick. They were terrorized but they started crying again when he was gone from their presence, though rather softly so as not to annoy him.

People generally evolve as their circumstances determine. Hussain had grown up as an orphan, suffering humiliation and beatings at the hands of others. His mother had died during childbirth and his father, a sea-pirate, had been killed in a fight with another gang. He was brought up by an uncle who beat him up almost every day. As a result, inflicting suffering on small children was something that came quite naturally to him. He never felt any remorse while doing so as this is how he himself had been treated when he was a small child.

One of the crew members took Hussain aside and advised him: "These children will die if you keep them much longer in the cargo area, and the entire effort of smuggling them out of India will go down the drain. Only one day has elapsed and a long journey still lies ahead. It is important that the children survive".

Hussain agreed to move the children to the deck. Once there, Sonu found things a bit more bearable. At least he could breathe better, something which had become difficult in the area where he had been kept earlier.

He tried to find out the names of the other children, but they spoke a different language and did not understand him; neither could he understand what they said to one another. These three boys had been kidnapped from the southern part of India. They spoke Tamil, a language entirely different from Hindi, the language which Sonu spoke.

After they had been at sea for another day, one of these other boys (who was roughly the same age as Sonu) became very ill. He had vomited several times and had thereafter gone off to sleep. Hussain tried to rouse him but found that the boy was in fact dead.

The little corpse was put in a sack along with some stones. The sack was then hurled into the sea and it disappeared under the water. The incident had a lasting impact on Sonu. He was unable to comprehend why that boy had been thrown into the sea.

However, he did comprehend that Uncle Vijay had snatched him away from his parents and placed him in the hands of some very cruel strangers who did not mean well towards him at all.

Nevertheless, Sonu was sure that his father would be able to find him soon and take him back to their house. His father would also punish Uncle Vijay as well as all these wicked persons.

The little boy, who was not even five years old was receiving a crash course in life's fickleness and randomness.

....and the ship of the desert

4

The '*dhow*' reached Dubai, a small port on the southern shores of the Persian Gulf. It was evening, and darkness would fall in an hour. The cargo was slowly unloaded, as also the three children who had survived the perilous voyage from India. Hussain handed them over to a man whom he addressed as Mohammad.

Mohammad paid him nine hundred rupees for each child.

Hussain cursed his luck and said to Mohammad, "I have lost nine hundred rupees as one child died during the voyage". Not for a moment did he feel any remorse. A young child had perished while in his charge, but the loss of nine hundred rupees was all that mattered to him.

Mohammad laughed and replied, "Make sure that all of them survive when you bring the next lot".

He took the three children to his Jeep which was parked some distance away. Then, he drove away with them into the desert.

Soon, it became dark and it was not easy to negotiate one's way through the desert terrain. However, Mohammad had traversed this route many times, during the day as well as at night.

The Jeep made its way forward leaving a cloud of sand and dust behind. A normal car would have got stuck, and only a four-wheel drive with an experienced driver like Mohammad could successfully negotiate its way ahead.

The three children in the Jeep were scared and anxious as they did not know where they were going; the ride was very bumpy and at times even more frightening than their voyage at sea. All around there was complete darkness.

After driving for about half an hour, they reached their destination. Mohammad alighted from the Jeep and gestured to the three boys to get down.

Sonu felt so weak that he was barely able to get up. Mohammad helped him and the others to get down and took them into a small shack made from corrugated iron sheets.

A smell of stale sweat pervaded the air inside.

In the light of a small oil lamp which burned in the shack, Sonu saw that two other boys were already lying there on the floor.

He thought that their appearance was very dirty; he did not realize that they thought quite the same about him. He could only see himself as the neatly groomed child whom he would often see in the mirror in Chandrapur— so unlike these urchins who lay in the shack. He had no idea that he was already like them---unkempt and dirty.

Mohammad left Sonu in this shack; he then took the other two boys with him.

❑ ❑ ❑

One of the boys in this shack was about the same age as Sonu, while the other one was a little older and bigger. Sonu found that he could communicate with these boys; this was because they spoke Urdu, which he could understand as it was quite like Hindi.

He felt happy on this account, as he had not been able to converse with the other boys who had travelled with him on the ship. Sonu felt less lonely now than he had done during the sea voyage.

Communication is such a bridge over troubled waters!

The older boy told Sonu, "My name is Naseem, and my brother's name is Waseem. We are from Pakistan".

He continued, "We had been sold by our parents to another Pakistani who brought us here. Our parents were tricked into thinking that we would work in some rich person's house and would live in comfort; they never realised that we would be brought to this place which is worse than hell".

Sonu asked, "When did you come here"?

"We have been in this camp for over a year", Waseem said, adding, "Some others have been here much longer". He began to cry as he said this.

Waseem asked him, "Are you from Pakistan or India"? Sonu could not answer as he did not understand what the question meant.

He could only tell them, "I am from a place very far away, and which is very different from this place".

Naseem remarked, "The place where we came from was also very different. There cannot be any place worse than this in the whole world".

He told Sonu: "Like us, you will also have to live here for the rest of your life. You will never be able to see your parents again".

Sonu shook his head and replied, "No, my father is a very strong man. He will come here and take me away".

He was sure that quite soon, his father would be able to find out where he was and come and rescue him.

Naseem asked, "Are you hungry"?

Sonu nodded, and Naseem said, "I will give you something". He opened a small box lying in a corner of the tent and brought two small pieces of bread. He also brought some milk in a glass.

Sonu took a piece of bread and put it in his mouth; it was hard, quite unlike the soft home-baked '*roti*' which his mother used to give him. He did not like the bread, but he ate it as he was hungry.

Then he ate another piece. So early in life, he was learning the rather painful lesson that beggars cannot be choosers.

Then, Sonu took a sip of the milk and almost vomited. It tasted very different from the milk in his house in Chandrapur, and he hated it,

"It's horrible", he said.

Naseem explained that it was camel's milk.

Sonu asked "What is a camel"?

Naseem was surprised at Sonu's query and said, "I will show you tomorrow what a camel is. Not a day will pass here when you don't see it".

Sonu had arrived at a turning point and would soon discover the big role that camels were going to play in his life.

❑ ❑ ❑

Sonu was very exhausted, and he could hardly keep his eyes open. A few sheets were spread on the floor. He lay down and was soon fast asleep. The village appeared in his dreams: the big house with a garden in front where he had lived till a few days back; his parents; his toys; the servants of the house with whom he used to play; the green landscape which he could see when he stood in the verandah, his father by his side.

He dreamt of all these things as he slept on a dirty sheet in a shack in an arid desert where life was so different from the comfortable home of his parents.

Dreams are such an escape from realty!

When Sonu got up in the morning, he saw that the other two boys were already up. His body still ached from the tough sea voyage, as also from having slept on the floor.

Sonu stepped outside. There were several such shacks nearby, with a barbed wire fence separating them from the vast desert all around. There were several other children hanging around, all of whom looked dirty.

Not far from the shacks, there was another area which had been fenced, and inside it there were some large animals. They appeared very strange, and Sonu felt scared of them. He went back to his shack.

Sonu asked Naseem, "What are these big animals which I saw outside"?

Naseem smiled and said, "They are camels".

"What are they doing here? Will they attack us"? Sonu was quite frightened.

Naseem said, "Never go near them on your own as they are wicked and can hurt you", adding, "a few days back a camel had bitten away the fingers of one of the boys".

He also told Sonu "We all have to ride on them. You will also have to do so. It is a very scary experience, as you will find out".

The hand of fate had brought Sonu to this arid desert to be a camel jockey!

❏ ❏ ❏

The camel camp where he was now living was called an '*ousbah*'. There were many shacks in the camp. Most of the children living in them were from South Asian countries, either kidnapped from their homes like Sonu or bought from impoverished parents who sold their children for just a few hundred rupees, hoping that a better life awaited them in some distant land.

For centuries, camel racing has been very popular in many Arab countries, especially those in the Gulf region. Derived from a Bedouin tradition, camel racing slowly evolved into a popular spectator sport which carried lavish prizes.

Children came to be regarded as the preferred camel jockeys as they are light in weight. Several thousand Asian and African children were trafficked every year and brought to Arab countries to become camel jockeys, and they fetched a good bounty for the traffickers.

The outside world was quite unaware that such a cruel and pernicious form of child slavery was in existence, and that it involved such un-describable abuse of the hapless victims.

As Sonu was going to discover, camel jockeys would be made to work for as many as sixteen hours every day. At the same time, they were deliberately underfed--nothing more than a few pieces of bread, some camel milk and occasionally some biscuits to keep their weight as low as possible. If a boy gained weight, it could spoil his chances of winning races.

Thus, like the other boys, Sonu was going to be subjected to a grueling schedule accompanied by deliberate underfeeding.

47

Besides, camels could pick up speeds up to forty-five miles per hour, and the consequences for a small child falling from a camel which was racing at a high speed are not hard to imagine.

Naseem said, "Many of the children are thrown off by the camels and get seriously injured; some even die as a result".

Amidst tears, he added, "We are slaves and must do whatever we are told. We have no choice at all".

❑ ❑ ❑

Mohammad and the other trainers in the '*ousbah*' had no qualms whatsoever about enslaving these young children and inflicting suffering on them. Their ancestors had been pirates and slave traders who attacked ships and raided other coasts to capture slaves. Enslaving and subjugating weaker persons was in their genes. Only this fact could explain how they could be so utterly cruel towards all the little children in the camp.

After enduring the trauma of being separated from his parents and forcibly brought here by ship, Sonu found that like all the other boys in the camp, he was now going to have to work from day break till night. They would be woken up at five in the morning. If any boy did not get up, his trainer would hit him with a stick and shout at him, calling him a '*kalb*' (dog) or '*khanzeer*' (pig).

Once he had woken up, he would have to clean the camp along with the other boys; this also meant cleaning the camel dung with his bare hands.

Later in the day, the boys would be trained in camel riding. Sonu came to dread this daily ordeal the most. He would be made to mount a camel which was seated on the ground and tied to it with a rope. Then, Mohammad would shout something in Arabic and hit the camel with a stick, whereupon it would start getting up.

Once it had got up, Mohammad would again hit the camel with his stick and it would start to run; soon, it would attain a good speed.

Sonu would cry out of fear, but there was nothing else he could do about it. Sometimes, he would learn that a boy had fallen from the camel and got seriously injured, or even died.

Sonu was among the smallest and lightest children in the camp, and Mohammad would give him very little food as he was determined to make sure that he did not gain any weight. Hunger would now be his constant companion, and far from being fussy in matters relating to food as he used to be at home, he was now like a hungry animal, devouring every morsel thrown to him.

"See how quickly this dog eats the food I give him", Mohammad said as he laughed wickedly.

Often, Sonu used to cry when he felt the pangs of hunger, and he would beg Mohammad for food, but the latter would beat him up, saying that every time he cried, this is what he would get instead of food. All the other boys were meted out the same treatment.

As the days went by, he began to lose any hope of being able to get out of this place.

"Why has my father not come to take me back'? Sonu asked Naseem one day.

Naseem replied, "Because your father does not know where you are. This place is so far away from where he lives".

❑ ❑ ❑

Sonu would often sit by himself and think about his parents. Hope had been gradually replaced by despair as realization began to sink deeper every day that his father would not be able to rescue him from this terrible place. He would have to endure such suffering for the rest of his life; perhaps he too would fall during the races and get trampled by the camels.

Sonu would cry as he thought of all this. When Naseem saw him crying, he would comfort him and tell him not to lose hope.

One night, when Sonu was sleeping, Mohammad woke him up and told him to come to his tent. He gave him some sweets. Then, he asked him to lie face downwards on his bed. Suddenly, he pulled down Sonu's pajama.

Sonu did not understand what was happening. Mohammad lay on top of him, and Sonu felt an excruciating pain. He shrieked, while Mohammad continued pushing him down.

The pain was unbearable, even worse than what he had to undergo during the day when riding camels would make his backside sore.

After a while, Mohammad got up. He told Sonu to wear his pajama, go back to his shack and not say a word to anyone or else he would beat him.

Sonu was crying; he could hardly walk as he felt great pain. He had no idea why Mohammad had punished him in this manner.

On many more occasions after that, Sonu would be taken by Mohammad to his tent, given sweets and subjected to the same treatment. He could not understand what was happening, and why was he being made to suffer such great pain which lingered for days on end. He was confused: why was he being given sweets and made to suffer pain at the same time?

One day, when Sonu came back from Mohammad's tent, Naseem saw that his pajamas had blood stains at the back.

He cursed Mohammad, calling him names and saying that Allah would send him to hell. Naseem knew what he had done to Sonu, as he had done the same to himself also, as well as to Waseem and many other children.

He also knew that the other boys in the camp had also been treated in this way by their trainers; if they objected, they were mercilessly thrashed.

Sonu feared and hated Mohammad more and more with each passing day.

❑ ❑ ❑

Soon, the big day arrived when the races were to be held. All the children from the camp were dressed up in different colours. This was done to identify their respective teams as well as the owners. All of them were assembled together in a large open space where there were many camels sitting on the sand.

Mohammad lifted up Naseem and seated him on a camel. Sonu could make out that Naseem was quite scared though he was trying his best to hide his fear.

"Are you scared"? Mohammad teased Naseem as he tied him to the camel. Then, one by one he seated Waseem, Sonu and all the other boys on different camels; he tied all the little jockeys to their mounts with ropes.

If any of the boys showed resistance, Mohammad would taunt them or even hit them gently with his stick.

Most of the other boys were crying, and Sonu also began to cry.

Mohammad made all the camels get up one by one. His team of camels and jockeys was now ready for the first race, which was going to begin shortly.

Likewise, the other teams also got ready for the race.

All the camels were then lined up next to each other. It was an unbelievable sight—at least forty camels with children perched atop, dressed in different colours.

Then, there was a gun shot, after which the camels began to run. It was a terrifying experience, and Sonu began to cry aloud. Most of the other boys were also crying and howling with fear, which pleased the trainers as they believed that the sounds made by the children in fact made the camels run faster.

The camels ran past hundreds of spectators wearing Arab attire who were all cheering and shouting.

There was a great din with the children crying, spectators shouting and the bells on the camels jingling as they raced along. Sonu could not see anything at all as tears were streaming from his eyes. He kept crying while his camel kept running.

Sonu was sobbing uncontrollably as his camel slowed down and stopped. The next thing he knew was that the camel was sitting down, front legs first and then the hind legs.

Mohammad untied him from the camel and Sonu found himself standing on the ground, his legs shaking from the experience. He saw that all the other camels were also sitting down and the children alighting from them. There was a lot of crying and howling all around.

Suddenly, Sonu was patted on the head by an old man who seemed to be overjoyed. Mohammad was also looking very pleased, and the old man and Mohammad hugged each other.

The reason for their joy and celebration was because Sonu's camel had won the race!

Sonu and all the children were quickly tossed into Jeeps and taken back to the starting line-up to take part in the second race.

He went through the ordeal of being tied to a camel again and again and made to take part in many races; when it was all over, he could not remember how many times he had gone through it.

Neither Sonu nor any of the other boys got any sort of reward for winning a race. The only thing which all of them would take back from the races were the memories of their horrible experience.

In fact, it had been the most frightening day in Sonu's life as he had seen many children falling from camels.

Sonu came back to his shack. Waseem was not there, and Naseem was crying uncontrollably.

Sonu asked him, "Why are you crying? Did you get hurt during the races"?

Naseem said that he was crying for his brother Waseem.

Amid sobs, he told Sonu, "Waseem fell from his camel and died as he was trampled by the camels coming from behind. Mohammad had buried him in the desert far away from the camp".

Sonu did not know how to console Naseem. He came and sat down near him and started crying too. Neither of them ate anything that night.

During the sea voyage, Sonu had seen how a boy died and his body was thrown into the sea. This time, he did not even see what happened to Waseem. He just became a memory.

That night, Sonu cried a lot, as he became even more convinced that sooner or later it would be his turn to fall, get crushed under charging camels and die in a horrible, bloody manner.

Several races were held during the next few weeks. Each time, Sonu and the others went through the same terrifying experience.

He would hear from Naseem about the horrible accidents which continued to occur in the camp, especially during the races.

Naseem would cry each time this happened, as he would be reminded of the tragic fate that had befallen his brother Waseem. He would also curse Mohammad and the other camel trainers, saying that he hoped that Allah would punish all such wicked people for the atrocities committed by them.

Thus, Sonu's ordeal continued unabated; he saw many children fall from the camels and die. Some others survived the fall but were crippled; they were taken away from the 'ousbah' and never seen again. The trainers considered such children useless and left them to die in the desert.

❑ ❑ ❑

Sonu had been enslaved in the *ousbah* for around six months, when one night, as he was asleep, Naseem woke him and said in a hushed voice, "I have noticed that there is a small gap in the fence which surrounds our camp. I am going to try to escape through that and run away". He added, "You should also come with me"

Sonu asked, "Will we not be caught"?

Naseem answered, "There is no sense in continuing to live in this place which is worse than hell. Even the camels here live better than we do".

Naseem was the only person in the camp whom Sonu trusted; he was the only one whom he turned to when he was sad, the only one on whose shoulder he could cry. What would he do if Naseem was not there to comfort him?

Therefore, he decided to do as Naseem said.

Naseem, too was very affectionate towards Sonu. After Waseem's tragic death, Sonu had somewhat filled the void in his life. He felt a certain responsibility towards him, as if he was his kin, for they lived together in the same tent, ate together and went through the same suffering day after day.

All was quiet in the camp. Everyone was asleep, and there was darkness all around. Naseem took some bread, wrapped it in a piece of cloth and gave it to Sonu to carry. He also filled some water in a bottle, put it in a bag and slung it across his shoulder.

Then, he told Sonu, "Follow me". They slipped quietly out of the shack towards the fence. Then, they sneaked out through the gap and ran into the dark, eerie night leaving the camp behind them.

□ □ □

Sonu was prepared to go wherever Naseem took him, for he was the only one in the 'ousbah' whom he felt close to. As for Naseem, he did not care where they were going, so long as they could flee from the camp, and from all the suffering that was inflicted there.

They trudged in the desert for over an hour. Sonu felt completely exhausted and pleaded, "I want to rest. I am too tired".

Naseem told him, "We must go as far as possible from the 'ousbah' as Mohammad will look for us when he wakes up and realizes that we are missing", adding, "On an earlier occasion, another boy had run away but Mohammad had been able to find him, after which he had beaten him so mercilessly that the boy could not even get up from his bed for many days; in fact, he died within a few weeks of the incident and his body was left somewhere in the desert".

Sonu asked, "Why did we run away if this could be our fate too"?

Naseem replied, "If we are caught, then perhaps we will be beaten and killed; it is better if our suffering is ended once and for all, so that we do not have to undergo such pain and humiliation everyday".

Sonu wondered whether such a risk was worth taking? He shuddered at the thought of what would happen if Mohammad was able to find them.

They both sat down, ate some bread and drank water.

Naseem said, "We should get up and travel as far as possible before sunrise".

They walked and walked till Sonu's feet ached with unbearable pain. Crying aloud, he said "I cannot walk any more. Go without me".

Naseem said softly, "Sit down and have some more water".

Then, they got up and walked again. This pattern of walking, resting and then walking again continued all through the night.

❑ ❑ ❑

At dawn, when he came to wake up the children, Mohammad discovered that Naseem and Sonu had fled, and he wanted to go in his Jeep and look for them in the desert. However, the wind that was blowing had erased their footprints in the sand, and he did not know which direction they had taken.

"These dogs will suffer and die in the desert", he said angrily to some of the boys who had gathered around him. "How far can they go on foot? Sooner or later, they will collapse in the sand, die and be eaten by the vultures. I gave them food as also a safe place to live. What will they get in the desert but starvation and death"?

He laughed aloud, for he was sure that they would meet such a fate.

"Of course, I will need to get replacements, but this will hardly be any problem", he boasted, "I can easily get as many such boys as I want from India, Pakistan, Iran and many other countries. You shall see how quickly I will get them".

❑ ❑ ❑

By day break, Naseem and Sonu had trudged quite far from the camp.

"Where are we going" Sonu asked? He felt scared, as there was nothing but the vast emptiness of the desert all around.

"I do not have any idea, but we should just keep going until we reach somewhere", Naseem replied.

Soon, the sun was very bright, and it was starting to get hot out there in the desert. The water which Naseem had brought along was finishing; only a little bit was left in the bottle.

Sonu said' "I am very thirsty. My mouth is completely dry".

Naseem told him to finish whatever was left in the bottle. Sonu asked him to have some too, but there was so little left that Naseem told him to have it all.

They walked on and on, and nothing was in sight but the desert all around.

Suddenly, Naseem shouted with joy. He could see water ahead. He pointed towards it and then started running in that direction. Sonu came slowly behind him; he could not run as he was totally exhausted.

There was no water, and it was only a mirage. The desert had beguiled them, as it had done to countless others before them.

Having made this burst towards the mirage, Naseem was totally drained of strength, and he just collapsed on the sand. Sonu came slowly behind and sat next to him.

He tried to make Naseem get up, but his efforts were in vain. Sonu had seen some children in the camp who had fallen from a camel. Like them, Naseem was lying completely still.

He felt even more lonely and scared than ever before. He did not want to perish here in this place, so he tried to get up and walk again. He had trudged only a few more yards when he felt that he could go no further. He looked up and saw that some birds had begun to hover in the sky above. Sonu was afraid of them; he had seen them once before when a dead camel had been dragged and left some distance away from the camp. He had seen how the birds had devoured the entire camel within a couple of hours!

Sonu's fears were well founded. Vultures were coming.

Homeward bound?

5

Mathew looked at the high waves and thought: "It is not normal for the sea to be so rough in March. Why is the weather so unusual for this time of the year"?

For centuries, small ships with masts and sails had sailed between ports in Kerala and the Persian Gulf. While the Arabs called them '*dhows*', people back home in Kerala called them '*Uru*', meaning a 'fat boat'. He had seen many such ships being built from teak wood in Beypore, a village south of Calicut. Later, the demands of modern day shipping had resulted in these ships becoming motorized.

For over ten years, he had been sailing on the route between Cochin and the ports in the Persian Gulf. He had gone on his maiden voyage accompanying his father to Kuwait. In a few years he would be taking his nephew Joseph and introducing him to the sea routes on which many generations of his family had sailed. He thought to himself that it was amazing how time had flown by.

During his voyages, Mathew had made countless friends in the ports and fishing villages to which he sailed. He was a devout Christian, an adherent of the Marthoma Church which was founded by Saint Thomas, one of the Apostles of Jesus Christ. His family had been Christians as far back he could trace his roots. However, religion never became a barrier in his relations with the Muslim population of these fishing villages. A tradition of mutual respect had developed between them, and Mathew was always welcomed in all these villages not just as a friend but in fact as a much-loved brother.

His small ship had arrived three days ago at Dubai; the cargo of rice which he had brought had been unloaded the very same morning, after which the cargo of dates had been loaded for the return journey.

He could have sailed back to Cochin the very next day. That is what most other ship-captains would have done. However, his relations with the people here were so close that he did not wish to leave so quickly without spending at least a couple of days with them. Neither would they be happy if he departed so soon.

Mathew was always touched by the affection shown to him by the Arabs who lived here. He felt totally at home here and simply loved their company.

He also knew that he would not return here before another year; other ports had to be visited in the coming weeks, after which the monsoon would set in. There was no question of sailing to the Gulf ports before the monsoon got over.

In short, Mathew decided that he was not going to start his return journey right away. "Let's enjoy the company of our friends here for a couple of days", he told himself.

"The weather is a bit rough and venturing out to the sea right now is perhaps inadvisable", he said to his sailors, adding "We will dock here for some time".

This is how he had stayed on longer than would have been necessary. In later years, he would wonder whether it was some unseen power which had kept him there for those two additional days.

❑ ❑ ❑

During these two days he visited one friend after another and drank countless cups of Arabic coffee; it was different from the coffee back home, and he liked both. He had brought for them gifts of cardamom which was grown in such abundance in Kerala; they would brew it with coffee and prepare an incredibly delicious drink which they called '*qahva*'.

On each of the evenings he spent there, Mathew sat with his friends near the shore and chatted, watching the fresh catch from the sea being grilled. When it was done, they ate it with rice till they were full, and then lazed around on the shore looking at the vast emptiness of the sea which seemed even more mysterious at night than during the day.

He had brought from his ship some arrack, a strong, alcoholic drink which is popular in Kerala. Though his friends were devout Muslims, they did not object to his having alcohol; in fact, a couple of them joined him in consuming the strong brew.

"What a great time I always have with these wonderful people", Mathew thought as he retired for the night.

❑ ❑ ❑

Before joining his forefather's profession as a sailor, Mathew had served for fifteen years as a constable in the Mounted Police Unit of Kerala Police. During this phase, he had become an accomplished horseman and had won many prizes in equestrian events in the National Police Games. He always sought an opportunity to indulge in his passion for horse-riding whenever he visited the Gulf ports. He felt that Arabian horses were the very best, and he loved to borrow a steed and ride away into the desert, leaving a cloud of dust behind him. His friends, too did not mind lending their horses to him as their experience had shown that he could handle any horse with consummate ease; they all agreed that Mathew was a very good rider.

Back home, he did not get much opportunity to ride, for once he was back in Cochin for short spells in between his sea voyages, all his time would be taken up by visits to numerous relatives and friends. Mary, his wife who had ruled him for over ten years was an inexhaustible socializer. No sooner would he return from a voyage than she would start drawing up a full calendar of engagements, and he had no option but to go with her wherever she wanted.

In other words, if he wanted to indulge in his passion for horse-riding, the time to do so was whenever his ship was anchored at ports such as Dubai.

His friend Abdullah had offered to let him ride the lovely mare *Hawa* (meaning 'the wind') which had been acquired by him recently. He had praised the mare so much that

Mathew could hardly wait for day break when he would mount her and ride away into the desert.

Mathew slept rather well that night. In fact, the arrack along with the fish and rice which he had consumed made him sleep more than he had intended to do. He had wanted to be up at daybreak, but it did not quite turn out that way. After making its appearance on the horizon, the sun had advanced quite a bit on its trajectory by the time he opened his eyes.

However, it did not take him long to get ready. Soon he was all dressed up, and off he went to get the mare from Abdullah.

Hawa was as good as Abdullah had claimed, and Mathew enjoyed riding her for around half an hour until he approached a small oasis. He decided to take a break there. It was becoming hot, and both he and *Hawa* needed to take rest and have some water.

He was gathering some dates which had fallen from a tree when he looked up at the sky and saw some vultures hovering above at some distance from the oasis. Had an animal died? Or, was it a human being? Mathew was somewhat curious, and he decided to find out.

In an instant, he was back in the saddle and was riding at full speed in the desert. He could see that the vultures were starting to get closer to the ground.

Mathew always kept a hunting gun with him whenever he ventured out into the desert. He fired the gun in the direction of the vultures, not to shoot any but to scare them. In an instant, they had all scattered away in different directions.

Mathew approached the place where the vultures had been hovering and saw that two small boys were lying there at a short distance from one another. He got down and examined the first boy. There was no pulse; the boy was dead. He walked over to the other boy; he did have a pulse, though a very weak one. The boy was alive, and he needed to be saved.

Mathew rushed across, got his water-bottle from the saddle and sprinkled some water on the boy's face. The boy moved, though only faintly. He put the bottle to the boy's lips, and he drank the water slowly, then a bit more, and then more.

The boy opened his eyes and tried to look around. "Naseem", he seemed to ask. Mathew knew that the boy was enquiring about his friend. He took him in his lap and showed him the inert body lying nearby. "Naseem", the boy started howling, "Naseem, Naseem". Mathew tried to console him.

Then, he decided that the dead child had to be buried. He dug a pit in the soft sand and buried the body.

With the young boy seated on the saddle in front of him, he rode back towards the oasis. He wanted to talk to this child and find out where he had come from, and what he was doing in the desert.

❑ ❑ ❑

Mathew was from Kerala where the language spoken is Malayalam. However, he had been watching Bollywood movies since long and had thus picked up enough Hindi, the language spoken in north India.

Besides, his voyages took him frequently to Mumbai, and he had made several friends there who spoke north Indian languages.

Thus, without much difficulty, Mathew was able to talk to the little boy and ascertain that his name was Sonu. "In that case, he must be from India", he thought.

Mathew asked, "What are you doing here in the desert"?

The little boy said, "I ran away with my friend Naseem last night".

Mathew asked, "From where did you run away"?

Sonu said, "I ran away from the camel camp. Life there was unbearable, and I would never like to go back to that horrible place".

"Where is the camp located"?

"There", he replied, pointing towards the desert.

"Please don't take me back to that place", he pleaded. "If you do so, Mohammad will surely beat me to death.

Mathew patted the child and assured him, "I will not do so. Don't worry".

Mathew asked, "Where did you live in India"?

"In the village", the boy replied.

"Which village", Mathew asked?

The boy looked puzzled. "Village", he said again.

He said, "I lived in a big house in the village".

Mathew realized that he did not know the name of his village as he was so young.

He asked, "What are the names of your father and mother"?

Again, the boy could not give a proper answer, saying merely that he called them *Babuji* and *Amma*; this is what many children in north India called their parents.

Mathew said to himself, "This boy is very young, and it is not surprising that he does not know the names of his parents or that of the town or village where he comes from". He asked him, "Did you run away from your house"?

The boy replied, "I did not run away. I love my father and mother a lot, and they love me too". He was so weak that he was struggling to speak. "I went with Uncle Vijay for a ride in his car. He took me home, and then his friend took me to his house. I don't know what happened, as I went off to sleep. When I woke up, I was on a ship with some very bad men".

Mathew knew from what the boy told him that he had been kidnapped by a relative and had thus ended up in this desert.

Mathew decided that he would take the boy with him to the ship. There was no other option. If he left the boy with some friend in Dubai, it was certain that eventually he would be returned to the camel camp. Mathew shuddered to think about the consequences for this little boy if that happened.

They rode off to where the ship was anchored. Luckily, there were no idlers hanging around his vessel; it was almost noon, and people had retired to their homes as it was already quite hot. Mathew took Sonu aboard the ship and told his small crew, "Look after him and don't say a word to anyone". He also told them to get ready to lift anchor.

Then, he rushed to Abdullah's house, thanked him for letting him ride *Hawa* and said, "I will be leaving immediately as the weather is much better now. The sea might turn rough again, and hence it is better for me to leave before that happens". He bid Abdullah goodbye and rushed back to his ship.

Soon, the ship lifted anchor and was sailing on its return journey back to India.

❑ ❑ ❑

Sonu's sea voyage this time was quite different from the one which had taken him out of India. Mathew made him sleep on a mattress on the deck, and he did not dump him in the cargo hold as Hussain had done when he smuggled him out of India.

Sonu had a bath with the help of one of the sailors, and his clothes were also washed. He had not had a bath since leaving Chandrapur around six months ago. There was always a scarcity of water in the '*ousbah*', and bathing was out of question for the little jockeys living there!

He felt much better now, though the motion of the ship made his stomach churn and he did not want to eat anything. Mathew gave him some coconut water and dates, which he thought were easy to digest. From time to time he or one of his crew members would come and check how Sonu was faring, and whether he needed anything. Generally, they found the little boy to be asleep or just lying down—so exhausted was he!

After sailing for four days, the ship began to approach the coastline of Kerala. Mathew could see the coconut trees in the distance, and he longed to be back on shore. However, he wondered whether he would face problems in case the port authorities asked for Sonu's identity papers.

Mathew had an idea. The ship had a couple of small life boats which could be used by the sailors in case their ship ran into problems. These were small boats, not unlike the ones sometimes used by fishermen when they ventured out to sea by themselves or in teams of two or three.

He got a boat lowered onto the sea and boarded it along with Sonu. He then asked the crew to take the ship to Cochin and get the cargo unloaded.

Thus, while the ship sailed towards the port, he began to row the boat towards another part of the shore used by local fishermen.

A coast guard patrol boat passed by and found nothing unusual about Mathew and Sonu being out at sea in this small boat. They presumed that they were among the thousands of fishermen from the villages located along the coast who sometimes went out to the sea on their boats along with their children.

He rowed for about an hour; finally, the boat reached the shore. After a horrendous ordeal lasting over six months, Sonu was now back in India.

Though the little boy felt completely lost, he was certain that the camel camp was far, far away and that Mohammad would not be able to come and take him back from here.

He was also sure that soon, he would be re-united with his parents! He could hardly control his happiness.

✦ ✦ ✦

Part Two

*P*rior to 1969, it had not been compulsory in India to register the birth of a child with any Governmental or municipal body. For admitting children, schools relied on the word of the parents about the date of birth.

The Registration of Births and Deaths Act was adopted by the Indian Government in 1969 and only thereafter did it become obligatory to obtain a birth certificate from the designated authority.

She thought to herself, "Clearly, this boy was born before 1969, and I do not need a birth certificate for him. However, to be on the safe side, I will get a birth certificate prepared".

She had a relative who made various kinds of fake documents such as college degrees, marriage certificates and birth certificates. "I will ask him to help", she decided.

She was aware of the widespread prevalence of such fake documents. "The birth certificate could come in handy at some stage", she thought.

After a couple of days, her relative gave her a birth certificate purportedly from the local Government Hospital.

A few days later, she boarded the train along with the little boy.

He did not have any idea where they were going and asked whether she was taking him back to his parents.

She replied that she was trying to locate them.

She did not tell him what she really planned to do.

Of course, she knew that if she was caught, she would be in big trouble.

During the journey, they passed by farms which were being cultivated, as also countless villages.

The landscape was so different from the desert which had surrounded the camel camp.

The greenery reminded little Sonu of the place where he had lived as a small child.

He kept looking out of the window, hoping to see his house; he was sure that he would recognize it.

With each passing hour, he became more and more hopeful.

He longed for his father to lift him in his arms and hug him, and for his mother to cuddle him and kiss him on his cheeks.

She opened her hand bag and took out a paper. It was a birth certificate which she had got prepared.

It mentioned the following details:

Name of the child	*Sunny Thomas*
Sex	*Male*
Date of birth	*September 18, 1966*
Mother's name	*Rosamma Thomas*
Father's name	*George Thomas*

As is the normal practice, the certificate was dated September 18th, 1966, as if it had been issued on the date of the child's birth.

She read it again, smiled and put it back in her hand bag.

The little boy was no longer Sonu, for she had given him a new identity.

✦ ✦ ✦

A Rose and no thorns?

6

Mathew felt a sense of relief as he had rescued Sonu and brought him back to India without encountering any hitch. The images of the vultures descending from the skies were still fresh in his mind. What if he had not gone out riding that morning, or gone in another direction? He looked at Sonu and shuddered at the thought of what would have happened to this little boy had he not arrived there in the nick of time.

Mathew needed to find a place where Sonu could live whilst he made efforts to locate his parents. His own two-room house was too small to accommodate another child. He had two small daughters, and Mary had been urging him to find a bigger place, as the family needed a room for guests. However, he had not been able to find anything suitable because rents were high.

In short, he knew that Mary would not agree to let Sonu stay with them. She had a temper, and he was not prepared to risk a tongue lashing if she flew into one of her foul moods, which was certain to happen under the circumstances. He had no option but to try and find some other place where Sonu could stay.

He decided to ask Rosamma Thomas, or 'Rosy' as she was called. Perhaps she would be able to keep Sonu for a few days.

When she was in her early twenties, she had got engaged to his friend George who was also a sailor. They had been madly in love with each other.

However, fate had been unkind, and during a storm his ship had sunk at sea; George and all the others on board had drowned.

She had remained single, though over a decade had passed by; no one took the place in her heart which George had occupied. Her parents had introduced her to several eligible bachelors, but she had turned them all down.

Rosy lived by herself in a small one-bedroom house. She worked as a school teacher and did not have any social life. Mathew thought that if he asked her to take care of Sonu for a few days, she might agree.

Straightaway, after reaching the shore, he headed off to see Rosy. She was at home. It was Sunday, and the school was closed for the weekly holiday.

Mathew told her how he had found Sonu in the desert and narrated the tale about the boy's ordeal which he had heard from him. He also told her how Sonu was so lucky to have survived, as the other boy who also had escaped from the camel camp had died in the desert.

Mathew mentioned that he wanted to return the boy to his parents.

"How will you find out who his parents are, or where they live"? Rosy was curious.

Mathew replied that it might take a while as Sonu could give him no information which could help in finding them. He hesitantly asked her: "Can you keep this boy in your house while I make efforts to locate his parents?"

He was mightily relieved when she answered: "Don't worry. I will take care of him".

Mathew cautioned her: "You might be asked questions about Sonu—Who is he? Where has he come from? Why does he not speak our local language Malayalam? Why have his parents not come with him? How long would he be staying stay here"?

He suggested, "You should merely say that he is the son of your friend who lives in Bombay, that he will be staying here for a few days after which he would go back".

Mathew made a quick trip to a nearby shop and bought some clothes for Sonu, as the boy only had what he had been wearing since the time he had found him in the desert. He gave the clothes to Rosy, after which he took leave of her and left for the port to see whether the unloading of the cargo of dates had been completed.

The Muslim holy month of *Ramadan* (or *Ramzan*, as it is known in India) was coming soon, and the dates would be in great demand as Muslims use them to break their fast; this is their universal practice.

The next few days were going to be very busy for Mathew, but he felt quite at ease as he had left Sonu in Rosy's charge. "She is a kind person. I am confident that she will look after Sonu quite well".

◻ ◻ ◻

Three days elapsed before Mathew could find time to visit Rosy again.

"I am leaving on a voyage to Muscat after four days and will return from there after two weeks", he told her. "I feel guilty about having asked you to look after this boy; after all, you are a busy school teacher and have a heavy work load of your own. I have no idea how to locate his parents, so I plan to hand over the boy to the police today and ask them to do so. I am anxious to relieve you of this burden".

"So many questions are troubling me", Mathew continued. "What should I tell the police? Naturally, they will ask: Where did you find the boy? How did you bring him to India without any documents"?

"Would they believe my story? They could also ask me as to why did I not bring the boy to the police station as soon as I returned to India? Where had I kept him during the last few days? They might ask me to come again and again for answering their questions, and this may affect my departure for Muscat".

He also told Rosy that he did not want to bring her name into all this, as they would perhaps require her to come to the Police Station for questioning more than just a few times, adding, "You know, a Police Station is not a nice place for a lady to have to visit".

She replied, "Don't be in a hurry to do anything. I will look after him until you return from Muscat".

She also told him that looking after the child was no problem for her.

"Are you sure"? He asked her with disbelief.

She reassured him, "Please take your time. Don't worry about him".

Mathew was profusely thankful to her.

❑ ❑ ❑

Thus, another twenty days elapsed before he could visit Rosy's house again. He reached there in the evening, as she would be at school during the day time. However, she was not at home, and the house was locked; he wondered where she had gone.

He went there the next day, but found the house locked again. Therefore, he enquired from the old lady who lived next door whether she knew when Rosy would be back.

"Oh, she is not coming back here. She has left this house".

'What"? Mathew could not believe what he had just heard. "When".

"Five days back".

"Where did she go"?

"I don't know. She did not tell anyone".

Mathew thought that it was quite strange on Rosy's part to have done such a thing.

"What about this house"?

"She has vacated it. It was a rented place, as you would know. She had only a few furniture items of her own, and she sold them to the land-lord. They are still in the house".

Mathew could not believe that Rosy could leave just like that!

He wondered, "What has she done with Sonu? To whom has she handed him over".

He asked, "Did she go alone, or was anyone with her"?

She said: "A small boy had been staying with her, and she told me that he was the son of her friend. She took him along with her".

He was completely baffled as he thought, "She must be out of her mind if she thinks she can keep him! After a few weeks, people will begin to wonder who the child is, and where has he come from? If she says that he is her friend's child, then they will wonder why the child is staying with for so long and not returning to his parents".

Mathew was extremely perplexed as he thought about this matter all day long. "I think that she must have handed him over to someone—but to whom"?

At the same time, he also felt angry and upset with Rosy. "When I meet her next time, I will scold her for having done such a stupid thing as leaving her house without telling me where she was going".

Salaam Bombay

7

Not surprisingly, Mathew did not have any idea that Rosy was planning to quit her job in Cochin and move to Bombay. His sea voyages had kept him busy, and he had not kept in touch with her until recently when he had come to visit her along with Sonu.

In fact, for several months, Rosy had been scanning the Classified Advertisements section in newspapers to see if any position was available for a Primary School English language teacher in Bombay. She had always wanted to live in that city which was considered the most cosmopolitan place in India.

She had come across many advertisements and sent her applications, but without any luck.

One afternoon, when she was talking to some of her fellow teachers, she learnt that the Saint Thomas High School in Mumbai was undergoing expansion, and that a new branch was being opened; the school was run by the Marthoma Church. She made some discreet enquiries and procured the address of the school.

Rosy sent her application seeking a position in the new branch of the school. She drew attention to her ten-year long teaching experience while also mentioning that she, too was an adherent of the Marthoma Church.

Rosy thought that apart from her qualifications, this fact might also help her in getting selected. She was aware that quite often, having the requisite qualifications was not good enough; other factors also played their part.

Three weeks elapsed and Rosy had had still not received any reply to her application.

When she was almost beginning to lose hope, she received an envelope in the mail. It was from the Saint Thomas High School.

She was afraid to open the envelope and held it in her hand for a few seconds. Was it a rejection letter, she wondered?

Plucking up courage, she opened the envelope and read the letter.

She had been offered the job with a salary of 450 rupees a month and accommodation in the school compound! It was too good to be true, and she rubbed her eyes to make sure she was not dreaming.

Within a few days of getting this job offer, Sonu had come into her life. She had always wanted to adopt a child. "Is it not God's work", she asked herself?

The fact was that Rosy did not want that Mathew should hand over Sonu to the police. The more she thought about it, the more convinced she became that it would not be a wise thing to do. "The boy does not have any idea where his parents live, and it is unlikely that the police will do much to find them. He will probably end up in some terrible orphanage, or even worse, in the hands of traffickers", she said to herself.

In this background, Rosy had decided what she would do: she would blend into the anonymity of Metropolitan Bombay where no one knew her.

She also decided: "I will change the boy's name. From now on, he is not going to be called Sonu; I am going to call him Sunny, for he has brought back sunshine into my life".

❑ ❑ ❑

Rosy sold whatever furniture items she possessed for a song to her land lord, as it would have been quite expensive to transport them to Bombay. In any case, they were old and quite worn out.

However, she did not tell him or anyone else exactly where she was going. Though they were curious about this issue, she merely said, "I am moving to another city".

She booked a room in a small hotel in Bombay where she would stay while she took possession of the accommodation which the school was going to provide to her.

All set, Rosy along with the little boy boarded the train to Bombay

He fell asleep as the train chugged along; he dreamt that his mother was telling him to have milk, and that he was asking for tea instead. Then, suddenly the dream turned to a nightmare-- he was now sitting on a camel which was running so fast that he was falling from it; then Mohammad was asking him to take off his pajamas.

Sonu woke up from his sleep, crying. However, he realised that it was only a nightmare. He often had such nightmares.

He felt relieved and went back to sleep again.

❑ ❑ ❑

Rosy had explained to the little boy that he should never discuss his past with anyone, and that to protect him, she had changed his name to Sunny.

"Don't tell anyone who you really are", she told him, "for those bad people will come and take you back to the camel camp".

The little boy understood this point quite well; he would not do anything which would send him back to that hell from which he had so miraculously escaped.

"When will you take me back to my parents"? He asked her many times.

"I am trying to locate them", she replied. In fact, she had no intention of handing him back to anyone, not even to his parents.

"I have always wanted to adopt a child, and God has given me one", she said to herself.

She wondered whether she could pull it off, or whether her act of deception would be discovered. What if Mathew found out where she was now teaching?

The child's parents must also be searching for him, and they must have asked for help from the police. What if he was recognised by someone?

She knew that she could end up in prison for what she was doing. Though she meant well towards him, her act would be considered child-kidnapping.

❑ ❑ ❑

The day after her arrival in Bombay, Rosy went to meet the Principal of the Saint Thomas High School; their meeting went off better than she had expected.

The Principal, John Abraham was a tall, fair, bespectacled and soft-spoken man in his late fifties. Welcoming her to the school, he explained, "Since the school has just been started, things have not really settled down", adding, "You are going to teach English and some other subjects to the students of the primary classes".

"Thank you, Sir. I will do my best", she replied.

"I hope you were informed that you will be provided only a one room accommodation within the school premises", he said to her.

"Yes, Sir", she replied.

"The accommodation is small, you know", he explained.

"No problem, Sir. Only my son will be staying with me, and the accommodation is adequate for us". she said.

"Is your husband not going to live here", he enquired?

She replied in a faint voice, "He passed away three years back".

"Oh, I am sorry", he said with genuine sincerity. "What is your son's name"?

"Sunny Thomas", she answered in a *non-chalant* manner, adding, "I want to admit him in the school, Sir".

She was very happy when he informed her that the boy would get a waiver of half his fees, as this was a privilege extended to all the children whose parents were employed in the school.

"Thank you, Sir", she said as she closed her eyes for a moment, crossed her heart and thanked the Lord for being so kind to her.

Then, taking leave of the Principal, she went to the Admissions Office. The little boy had been waiting outside the Principal's office, and she took him along with her.

The admissions clerk was an elderly man named Paul.

He asked her to fill up the admission form giving the relevant details of the child.

She quickly filled up the form and handed it to him.

He glanced over it and gave her a payment voucher while confirming that only half the normal fees would have to be paid by her.

"Please pay the fees. Sunny can start attending school from tomorrow".

Rosy did not have to produce the birth certificate which she was carrying. However, she decided to keep it, in case the need for it arose sometime later. She was relieved that everything had gone off so smoothly on her first day at the new school.

Had a new chapter had begun in her life, as also that of the little boy?

□ □ □

Rosy quickly adjusted to her new school, as also to Bombay. The fact that she had been provided accommodation in the school premises made things easier for her than would have been the case if she had to stay somewhere else and shuttle between home and school by local train or by bus.

On the other hand, Sunny took time to adjust to formal education. Often, he had difficulty concentrating on whatever the teacher was saying as his mind would invariably take him back to his past.

He longed to get back to his parents. At the same time, his memories of the '*ousbah*' where he had suffered so much trauma including sexual abuse kept haunting him, as they had left such deep scars on his mind.

Rosy doted on the little boy as if he were her own son and did everything possible to keep him cheerful. She was aware that her foremost task was to make him adjust to formal education. She knew that this task presented big challenges; nevertheless, she was confident that it could be accomplished. She would tutor him as she alone could— by healing him emotionally. She was hopeful that once he started enjoying the process of learning, he might forget the ordeals of the past and concentrate on his studies.

To keep his mind fully occupied, and to prevent him from thinking about his traumatic past, she would play indoor games with him such as Ludo, Carrom and Snakes & Ladders. She knew that young children were very fond of such games. Thus, slowly but surely, she tried to divert his attention away from his painful memories.

Sunny began to do well in his studies. At the end of the school year, he got the first prize in his class, as also a special prize for Elocution. The latter had been a foregone conclusion, as no one in his class could recite nursery rhymes as well as Sunny; Rosy had coached him a lot in this respect.

The result at the end of the second year was identical. Rosy was very proud at the way he was shaping.

At the same time, Sunny continued to show great fondness for playing indoor games and would ask Rosy to teach him more such games.

It was thus that he began his love affair with chess.

Rosy's father had been the Kerala State Chess Champion for many years, and she had learnt the game from him. Although Sunny was just a small child, she decided to try and teach him this game.

He liked it more than all the other indoor games which she had taught him. Soon, he began to play chess with her every evening. She was amazed at how quickly he was becoming good at this game. In a few months, he could give her a reasonably tough fight.

"Very soon, you will defeat me at chess", she told him jokingly.

"I will become the best player in the world", he boasted.

❏ ❏ ❏

One day, Mary, who was one of her fellow teachers in the school told Rosy that she had recently visited some relatives in Dubai, a port-city in the United Arab Emirates, which was a new country which had been formed in December 1971. She said that she had learnt from her friends in Dubai that the ruler there, Sheikh Rashid was a far-sighted man, and that he wanted to transform this Emirate from a small cluster of fishing villages and settlements into a modern city.

She continued: "Lots of jobs have been created due to the Sheikh's policies, and I saw many Indians there.

While some Indians were engaged in private business, many others were employed in various capacities, such as doctors, engineers, accountants, managers and teachers".

Rosy listened to everything that Mary was saying without paying too much attention until she said "I think we should look for jobs there. The place seems to have a very bright future".

Rosy was taken aback, and she replied, "There is no way I am going to leave Bombay and go to Dubai. Bombay has all the facilities of a modern city, and what does Dubai have", she asked?

Rosy continued, "Dubai will never become a developed city like Bombay, and I will not leave this modern city and go to that small place in the desert".

Feeling somewhat disappointed, her friend changed the subject and their discussion about Dubai ended.

❑ ❑ ❑

When everything seemed to be going along smoothly, a development occurred which again changed life's course for Rosy, and thus for Sunny.

George Abraham, the elderly Principal of the Saint Thomas High School retired and was replaced by a younger one in his mid-forties whose name was William Chandy. He was a short, dark man who put generous quantities of coconut oil in his hair and would laugh hysterically at his own crude jokes which he would narrate in a loud, shrill voice. Rosy disliked him from the very beginning.

The problem, however, was that Chandy, who was a widower had taken a fancy towards Rosy, and he would call her over to his office on some pretext or another. Often, he would ask her some questions which were of a personal nature. The fact that they were both single seemed to have given him ideas.

Being a reserved person, she did not like his inquisitiveness and dreaded their encounters which, to her dismay, were becoming more and more frequent. One day, he even tried to hold her hand on some excuse! She pulled it away in anger, prompting him to mutter an apology.

Thus, Rosy was not comfortable with the idea of continuing in this school with Chandy as the Principal.

She told her friend Mary, "I have been thinking about whatever you had said the other day about Dubai. Please try to find out whether there is any opening for me there, for I would like to give it a try".

"I am happy that you have changed your mind", Mary replied. "I will make enquiries and let you know as soon as possible. God willing, we will both get good jobs there".

Within a fortnight, she was back with some news. "The Indian High School in Dubai is looking for teachers for the primary classes. The salary offered is four times what we are getting in Bombay".

She continued, "Dubai is undoubtedly a costlier place in comparison to Bombay, as everything has to be imported, including food items. Additionally, we will have to rent accommodation there, which we do not have to do in Bombay".

"Despite this, we will be able to save almost as much money in Dubai as the entire salary which we are earning here in Bombay; all Indians who go to work in Dubai are able to do so. We can work there for some years, save some money and then come back to India whenever we want to" she told Rosy.

Both prepared their respective applications addressed to the Indian School in Dubai and mailed them. Within three weeks of sending her application, Rosy received a letter offering her the job she wanted!

She had been appointed as the English teacher in the primary wing of the Indian High School, Dubai, and she was to join when the next school session started in the first week of September. Unfortunately, her friend's application was not accepted as another candidate was selected as the Maths teacher.

It was only April, and several months still lay ahead before she would start her new job. She was excited that she would be commencing a new life soon, and once this happened she would be rid of that insufferable Chandy!

She decided that she would not say a word to anyone at this stage. "As the old saying goes, there's many a slip between the cup and the lip", she told herself.

There was too much work to be completed in the meantime. First and foremost, she had to get a passport. She decided to apply immediately for it as it would take quite a few months to get one.

The passport office worked on Saturdays, which was good for Rosy as she would not have to take leave from school to go there. She filled out the application form and made her friend check it thoroughly before she deposited it there.

Sunny's birth certificate was attached to the application so that his name was included on her passport as a dependent minor to enable him to travel with her.

Three months elapsed before Rosy got her passport. Immediately, she sent her passport details to the Indian High School in Dubai, and within four weeks she had received her visa. She was now all set for Dubai.

Rosy booked her seat on the Air India flight to Dubai leaving on 30th August 1973.She resigned from the school and within a week, she and Sunny were flying from Bombay to Dubai.

She was understandably nervous about this new chapter in her life. It was a leap into the unknown, and only time would tell whether she had taken the correct decision in moving to that small city in the desert.

She was also aware that such a gamble had worked out quite well for some people, but not for all.

Despite his tender age, Sunny could comprehend that Rosy was taking him to a far-off place. He wanted to run away and start searching for his parents, but fear held him back.

He realized that he was too young to take up such a challenge on his own. "I will find my parents when I grow up", he told himself.

What he did not realise was that his new home would be just a few miles from that camp in the desert where he had spent several months enslaved as a camel jockey!

Fate was taking him back to Dubai again, and he could never have imagined what it had in store for him this time.

Would it heap suffering on him again? Or, would he be spared another ordeal?

✦ ✦ ✦

Another school?

8

The Indian High School in Dubai was established in 1961 in a one room tenement and with only eight students who were the children of Indian expatriates. It was the first such expatriate institution in that Emirate.

As the Indian population in Dubai expanded, so too did the School since it had to cater to the needs of the families which kept arriving from India.

Consequently, more and more teachers were needed to run the school; some stayed only for a few years as they were unable to adjust to the harsh climate of Dubai where, during summer temperatures could be as high as 50 degrees centigrade and humidity go up to 95 %.

However, by the year 1971 when the UAE was set up as a separate country, the school was a well-established institution with a high reputation.

Later, Sheikh Rashid, the ruler of Dubai granted a piece of land to the Indian school and it grew from strength to strength, with generous contributions from local Indian businessmen helping it along.

This was the school where Rosy would now be teaching after moving from Bombay, as also where she was going to admit Sunny.

Sunny was understandably troubled at finding himself in this new environment. The local people, dressed in traditional

111

Arab attire whom he would see every day constantly reminded him of Mohammad and the other trainers in the '*ousbah*'. He was scared to be in a place which constantly reminded him of his ordeal in the camel camp.

"Why have you brought me here? Mohammad will come and get me. Please, let us go back", he would beseech her. She would try to reassure him that no harm would come to him.

"How will I find my parents if we live in this place"?

Often, he would start crying in his sleep, for he would have nightmares that he was being beaten and sexually abused by Muhammad".

In Bombay, he had sometimes thought of running away from Rosy to find his parents, but he did not entertain any such ideas in this new place. Out of fear, he would clutch Rosy's finger whenever they went out. He was afraid of his new surroundings, and of the unknown.

❑ ❑ ❑

The day after reaching Dubai, Rosy reported to the school and met the Principal Dr. Jai Motihar, a grey-haired, smartly dressed Sindhi gentleman in his mid-fifties. He was happy to see her and asked how she felt about joining their school.

"I am really excited about my new job, Sir", Rosy replied enthusiastically.

She had taken along Sunny, and Dr. Motihar gave him a warm hand shake saying: "Welcome to our school, young man". Rosy thought to herself that it was the first time anyone had addressed Sunny as a 'young man', for he was not even seven years old!

The school session was to start a few days later. It was a very busy time for Rosy, who had to quickly settle down in a one-bedroom apartment which she rented in Karama, a residential area not far from the school. Many Indians lived in Karama, which she found quite reassuring.

She installed some basic furniture and bought some essential items, telling herself that most other things could be procured in due course after she started drawing her salary from the school.

❑ ❑ ❑

Rosy was fascinated by Dubai and would spend hours walking around its shopping areas. She found that many of the shops were owned by Indians, mainly Sindhis and became acquainted with many of them.

She learnt that after the partition of India and the creation of Pakistan in 1947, they had to flee from Sindh, leaving their homes and other properties behind. They had come to Dubai either directly or through India and had not only rebuilt their lives in a short span but had in fact prospered and become rich.

She would sometimes wonder, "Can I also become rich like them some day"? Then, she would dismiss such thoughts. "Don't dream", she would tell herself, "be realistic".

Rosy wondered why Indians here in Dubai drove better cars and were better attired than their relatives back home in India. Where had India gone wrong, and where was it heading? Why did people there have to wait ten years to get a simple scooter, and several years to get a telephone connection? Here in Dubai she had got a phone connection just two days after she applied for one.

She worried about these and many other matters; she was not alone, for almost all expatriate Indians in Dubai whom she knew had similar concerns. Her discussions with them often centered around how India could be made a better place for the common citizen.

However, more than anything else, Rosy worried about Sunny's future. She hoped that one day he would grow up to be a successful person—someone whom people admired and looked up to.

She coached him very diligently in his studies. She also spent a lot of her leisure time playing chess with him; he had now become a very good player and would invariably defeat her.

Sunny, too had an obsession which he shared only with Rosy: he would not be at peace until he could find his parents. Whatever happened, he would never give up his dream of being re-united with them.

❏ ❏ ❏

While Rosy could not take the place which his parents occupied in his heart, he needed her and felt unsafe without her. He could not get rid of the fear of being taken back to the camel camp from where he had escaped, for he knew that Mohammed would be extremely vengeful.

He did not know that the camp where he had been enslaved was situated only a few miles away from where he now lived.

Every day, he saw the local people in Dubai wearing the traditional Arab dress which Mohammed and the other trainers used to wear in the camel camp, and he would be filled with fear. What if one of these persons recognized him? What if they caught him and took him back to the '*ousbah*'? He shuddered to think about what would happen to him; he would be beaten and sexually abused as was the norm there. Sonu feared that maybe Mohammad would also kill him.

Sunny felt safe only when he was with Rosy. He would cling to her whenever he accompanied her to the market. He needed the security which she gave him. He would also beg her not to leave him alone at home even if she had to go out briefly for grocery shopping, as he was afraid that Mohammed would come and get him.

One day, he froze with terror, for he saw Mohammed standing in the parking lot outside his apartment building! Had he come to get him?

However, that man went away. Perhaps, it was not Muhammad but only someone else who looked like him from a distance.

Nonetheless, the fear of running into Mohammed would never leave him in such an environment. If Rosy was with him, he would have her protection—though at times he had nightmares in which Mohammed along with the other trainers from the *ousbah* would mercilessly beat him, and Rosy was unable to protect him as she was outnumbered. He would wake up screaming: "Don't beat me, don't beat me". Rosy would gently pat him and put him back to sleep.

However, Sunny need not have worried. His appearance had slowly changed a lot. He was now a smartly dressed and well-groomed young lad who looked completely different from the disheveled, dirty camel jockey.

He was no longer Sonu from the *'ousbah'*. He was now Sunny Thomas.

✦ ✦ ✦

Check mate!

9

Six years had passed by since their arrival in Dubai, and they had settled down quite well in this city. Sunny was continuing to do well in his studies. Rosy tutored him painstakingly and made sure that he was always amongst the best in his class.

With the passage of time, the fear of being captured by Mohammad and taken back to the '*ousba*h' had slowly faded away.

Sunny was going to pass out from school in three years, and Rosy wanted him to be admitted to some good college in America or in Britain. However, she did not have the funds to make this happen.

One day, she was thinking about this matter when she casually said to him, "If I have my own school, even if it is just a Kindergarten for small children, I will make enough money to afford good quality college education for you in the United States".

Rosy lamented, "This is wishful thinking, of course, as private schools in Dubai can only be owned by U.A.E. nationals". She knew that she could not own a school; she would need a U.A.E. national as her sponsor. According to the prevailing laws and practice, he would hold the majority stake while she would have to make the investment required for starting such a venture.

"Where will I find the money for this", she lamented?

Then, something happened which would be a game-changer, and which would have an enormous effect on their lives.

Sunny had slowly emerged as a very good chess player. Rosy was not surprised when he won the chess championship of the Indian High School in the Junior's category.

He went on to win the Inter School Chess Championship of Dubai in the junior's category for three successive years and continued his winning run by winning the senior category championship also, beating many players who were much older. He was selected to represent Dubai in the U.A.E Inter School Chess Championship, in which he won the first prize with consummate ease.

Consequently, he was selected to represent the U.A.E. in the World Inter School Chess championships to be held in London. No one gave him much chance as there were many experienced players in the fray.

However, he defeated highly ranked players in the League matches in his group, and then thrashed his Pakistani opponent in the semi-final.

He was now being acclaimed as a giant-killer. Still, no one gave him an iota of a chance in the final as his opponent was Vladimir Petrokov, the reigning World Champion from the Soviet Union.

However, Sunny was victorious in a tough three-game final which left experts astounded at his brilliant play!

Expectedly, the U.A.E. press was jubilant about his victory and hailed him as a super star.

A prominent and powerful Sheikh from Dubai's ruling family was the President of the U.A.E. Chess Federation. He had already begun to take notice of this young Indian boy who held so much promise, and who was bringing glory to the U.A.E. as well as to Dubai.

When Sunny won the World Junior Championship, the Sheikh organized a grand function to felicitate him. The Sheikh was well known for his passion for chess, as also for his generosity.

He told Sunny: "I have been very pleased with your success, and you have brought glory to Dubai and to the U.A.E. What help I can give you"?

The Sheikh meant to ask if Sunny needed any help such as better coaching facilities to continue improving his game.

After thinking for a few seconds, Sunny replied, "My mother teaches at the Indian High School, but she often tells me that her dream is to have her own school. Your Highness, I would be very happy if you could help her".

The Sheikh smiled, as he realized that Sunny had misunderstood his question. However, he had already been impressed with Sunny's success, and now he liked the lad even more because he had asked for something for his mother, not for himself.

The Sheikh asked for her name and said that he would see to it that her dream comes true.

There were hurdles, but the Sheikh was a true Arab royal; he had given his word to Sunny, and he was going to find a way out. Besides, he was a man who would go to any length to reward people whom he liked, and there was no doubt that he liked Sunny.

Moreover, being a shrewd person, he realised that there was the need for another school for the Indian community as its numbers were increasing day by day; such a school would be a sound business proposition also. Under Dubai law, he would hold the majority stake in this venture. He was sure that he would not only recover his investment in a few years, but also make pots of money in the longer run!

Sunny told Rosy about his meeting with the Sheikh. She could not believe what he said! It was too good to be true. Without any investment of her own, she could set up a school and would run it herself! She was thrilled beyond words!

Within a few weeks, she was asked by the Secretary of the Education Department to meet him.

During their meeting, he told her that the Sheikh had decided to sponsor her school and had also given her the land for setting it up.

"He has also given you an interest-free loan of five hundred thousand dirhams to construct the school building and other amenities," he told her. "Re-payment will commence after three years. All the legal formalities are also being taken care of".

Immediately after the meeting, she wrote a letter to the Sheikh and thanked him for his extraordinary generosity.

Within a few days, she took possession of the land allotted to her and obtained the loan. In remarkably quick time, the construction of the school also started.

She planned to construct only a small building, as she needed to stay within her budget. She could expand the building later when money came in through school fees, but she was in no hurry to do that. "We must go slowly but surely", she would often tell Sunny.

The small building was ready within a year and she was now all set to recruit teachers and staff, as also to advertise for students. Having been in the educational field for so long, she had the requisite experience for all these tasks.

Of course, she had already thought of an appropriate name for the school. It was going to be called 'New Indian High School'.

❑ ❑ ❑

The school was due to start in September 1984; Rosy was quite pleased, as it would coincide with the completion of

Sunny's schooling and his departure for college studies abroad. She could then devote all her time to running the school.

Sunny, however had made his own plans: he did not want to go to abroad for college studies at all!

He observed that in Dubai, there were many people who had not studied beyond school, and yet they had done better than people who had University degrees.

"Going to college is something I don't want to do, and this idea had been consigned by me to the garbage bin long ago", he told Rosy. "Why should I slog for four years in college, then go to someone who has not studied beyond school and ask him for a job which would pay me only a small fraction of what my employer himself would be making"?

Rosy was understandably quite upset. She had boasted to her friends that Sunny would go to some good American or British University, and if he discontinued his studies after school, she would be the butt of their jokes!

However, Sunny had decided that he was not going to study any further. He said: "I want to help you in running the school".

Sunny also told her quite vehemently, "Look, the teachers in the Indian High School have University degrees, but they earn a pittance in comparison with Seth Motwani (a board member of the school) who, perhaps has not studied beyond class ten! Even the Principal Dr. Jai Motihar earns less than what Seth Motwani gives as pocket money to his four sons, who are all students of the same school"!

Rosy grudgingly admitted that what Sunny was saying was true. Seth Motwani had come to Dubai on a boat with just a small suitcase containing nothing more than a few clothes; he had set up a small trading company and become a millionaire in less than ten years. He was enormously wealthy, lived in a palatial house and had a fleet of cars.

Rosy made one last effort: "Seth Motwani's lack of education shows up in a variety of ways, and many of the teachers of the school laugh at him behind his back. People also say that he has made all his money by smuggling gold to India! I don't want you to be like that. I want people to respect you".

However, Sunny had an answer for that as well: "It hardly matters what people say about Seth Motwani behind his back. What matters is that he has money, and that gives him power. Whatever people may think of him, they nevertheless accept his authority over them".

Sunny did not budge, and Rosy had to drop her plan to send him abroad for pursuing higher studies.

❏ ❏ ❏

'New Indian High School' started functioning in 1984 with just two hundred students spread over six classes from Kindergarten to the Fifth Standard. Rosy planned to expand the school building in stages and add at least one additional class every year.

Rosy had kept the fees quite low by prevailing standards, and this made the school affordable for many parents who could not send their children to more expensive schools.

As a result, the school began its operations at nearly full capacity from the first year itself.

Rosy soon realized that Sunny was indeed a great asset to her. For one thing, there was no one else whom she could trust one hundred per-cent. He was also very good at public relations, and the task of running the school needed this skill as it involved dealing not only with the parents and teachers but also with government departments to get various day to day problems sorted out.

Sunny had a flair for dealing with people, and he learnt all the tricks of the trade very quickly. For example, he would send birthday greeting cards to many key people in the Government whom he had to deal with; he would often carry a suitable gift when he went to meet these officials; and above all, he would make it a point to personally wish them on all important occasions such as *Ramadan, Eid ul Fitr, Eid al Adha* and of course the U.A.E. National Day.

These little gestures did not go unnoticed, and he would be treated with not just courtesy but also warmth by all such officials. Despite being so young, Sunny could cut through bureaucratic red tape like a proverbial hot knife through butter.

❑ ❑ ❑

As the years went by, both Rosy and Sunny got busier with the work relating to the school. This was a period of consolidation for them.

'New Indian High School' expanded every year, and by 1989 (just five years since it was started), it had become an institution where children could study from Kindergarten till Class Twelve, at which stage they finished their schooling and were ready to go to college.

The school now had more than two thousand students, and this number was expected to keep growing due of the continued influx of Indians to Dubai. The revenues of the school were also increasing every month. Now, Rosy and Sunny both drove their own luxury model cars.

In addition, within a few years of opening her school in Dubai, Rosy had received offers for setting up schools in Sharjah, Ras Al Khaimah and Fujairah.

A lot of her time, as also that of Sunny was being consumed in handling the school's workload which was growing at a very rapid pace. Each day brought fresh challenges, with decisions having to be made carefully and yet quickly.

❑ ❑ ❑

A characteristic of Indians living abroad is their desire to always keep themselves abreast of developments which take place back home. They follow not only political and economic developments in India but also those in other areas such as films and cricket.

Rosy was no different in this regard. Every day, she would read the 'Malayala Manorama', a newspaper from Kerala to follow whatever was happening in her home state.

One busy day, Rosy came across an item in the Obituaries page which immediately caught her attention. Mathew had died! The funeral had already taken place, but the Memorial Service would be held in the Marthoma Church in Cochin after five days.

With the passage of time, she had all but forgotten him, but the obituary filled her with guilt. She had left Cochin without telling him, and she knew that he must have been furious.

Though still in her fifties, Rosy was in failing health as she had been diagnosed with cancer. Perhaps as an act of repentance, she decided to unburden herself to Sunny.

She described all that had happened after Mathew had rescued him from the desert and brought him back in his ship.

Sunny listened to her with rapt attention. Though he did not say anything, he felt angry that she had run away with him to Bombay, without giving Mathew any chance to locate his parents through the police.

Sunny realised that he owed a huge debt to Mathew, for he would have died in the desert and got eaten up by vultures had Mathew not rescued him and then brought him back to India in his ship.

He decided to go to Cochin for attending the Memorial Service.

Even after his death, Mathew once again shaped Sunny's life in a decisive fashion.

After the Memorial Service, Sunny went to Mathew's house for the first time and met his wife and two daughters, Molly and Polly.

It was love at first sight for him. Sunny thought that Molly, the elder daughter was the most beautiful girl he had ever seen. Molly, too liked him a lot.

Six months afterwards, he and Molly were married in a simple ceremony at the Marthoma Church in Cochin.

Three months later, the cancer took its toll and Rosy died. Sunny was now all alone at the helm of his educational empire, though he felt happy that Molly was there by his side to help him.

During the next few years, Sunny set up schools in three other Emirates which had invited him to do so. Thus, by 1996, he was running schools in Sharjah, Ras Al Khaimah and Fujairah.

He established an educational management company under which all the schools would function and named it The PEARLS (Premier Education and Rapid Learning Syndicate) Group.

His vision was that one day his company would have a global presence. He wanted to set up schools in as many countries as he could.

The little boy who had been abducted from his home, enslaved in a camel camp and undergone such horrific suffering was now running an educational powerhouse.

Fate, which was so unkind to him at one time had dramatically changed course and made him a very rich and famous man. People now referred to him as 'Tycoon Sunny'.

❑ ❑ ❑

However, Sunny continued to be haunted by the memories of his childhood. Not a single day passed when he did not feel frustrated at his own inability to go back to his roots and find his parents. This made him restless and irritable; despite being wealthy, he was not at peace with himself.

Sunny's mind would keep going back to his infancy. He could clearly recall the faces of his parents. However, try as hard as he could, he was unable to remember their names or that of their village—that idyllic place where he had lived with them in those blissful years. This increased his sense of frustration. How on earth was he ever going to be able to find them?

Sunny noticed that Indian newspapers often carried classified advertisements about missing persons. He thought that it might be possible for him to locate his parents through a newspaper advertisement.

Accordingly, he placed an advertisement in the Times of India to the effect that a young boy named Sonu had got separated from his parents more than twenty years back; if anyone had any knowledge about his parents, then they could write to a certain post office box number in Dubai.

Several months passed by and there was not a single reply.

Sunny placed a few more such advertisements, but there was no response. He was frustrated at his inability to make any headway.

There had been so many twists and turns in his life. Could there be another one?

+ + +

There at last!

10

One country where he was encountering enormous bureaucratic hurdles was India. Though it had begun to seek foreign investments, there was a labyrinth of procedures and permissions which had to be gone through.

However, he was determined to overcome all such problems. He set up an office of The PEARLS Group in Cochin and made Polly, his sister-in-law in charge of it. He wanted that his company's first school in India should be set up in the city where he had landed after he had been rescued by Mathew. Sunny began to visit India quite frequently for the proposed school project.

It was on one such visit in 1996, when he was staying at the Taj Mahal Hotel in Mumbai that he came across a front-page report in the 'India Times' which mentioned that the villagers of Surajpur (located in the city of Allahabad in the state of Uttar Pradesh) had discovered the partially decomposed remains of a young girl buried on the farmhouse of a man named Mahinder Singh, who had been taken into custody along with his associate Joginder Singh.

The next day, he came across a more detailed report in that newspaper about the 'Surajpur Case' (as it was now being called). It described how the Police had conducted a thorough search and found many more skeletons of children buried inside the fenced compound of that farmhouse.

The report stated: "Police investigations have revealed that Mahinder Singh headed a criminal gang which was engaged in several activities such as the illicit liquor business, smuggling from Nepal, prostitution and child-kidnapping.

Several members of the gang have been arrested, but Mahinder's key accomplice named Vijay Bahadur Singh is absconding. The police have placed a reward of twenty thousand rupees on him".

A photograph of the absconder, Vijay Bahadur Singh was carried alongside the report.

Even after two and a half decades, Sunny recognized him---his hair had turned grey, but he was the very same Uncle Vijay who had taken him away from his parent's house that fateful afternoon!

He had never been able to forget the face of this man who was responsible for his ordeal and enslavement in the camel camp. It was his face that was now staring at him from the newspaper!

❏ ❏ ❏

Sunny knew that this was the vital clue which would help him find his parents. He decided immediately to go to Surajpur.

He flew from Mumbai to Delhi and then reached the New Delhi Railway Station just in time to catch the night train from there to Allahabad. The journey in the First Class Air-Conditioned Coach was quite comfortable. After a light dinner, he fell off to sleep only to wake up when the train reached his destination in the early hours of the morning.

The travel agent had booked his accommodation in the Grand Hotel, which was rated amongst the best in the city. After checking into the hotel, he went to the hotel's travel desk to engage a car and a driver to go to Surajpur.

It was late morning when he started his journey on the pot-holed and bumpy road. The distance which he had to cover was less than thirty kilometres, but the road was often quite narrow and congested.

His heart was beating faster than it had ever done before; the excitement was quite unbearable.

Soon, the car was outside the city limits and was winding its way through the countryside. It was spring, and the agricultural fields were green and yellow with the mustard crops that were ripening there.

Sunny remembered such a landscape from his childhood; when his father would lift him up in his arms, the farms would look just like the ones which he was now passing by.

He was struck by the beauty of these farms. They were so different from the arid, brown landscape of the desert around Dubai. India was so blessed, yet it was poor. Sunny felt sad that this was so.

After an hour, they reached Surajpur. Sunny asked his chauffeur, whose name was Dilip to approach some locals gathered at a tea shop and get the directions to Mahinder Singh's house where the police had discovered the remains of many children.

They presumed that Sunny was a journalist who was tracking the story which had given Surajpur such a notorious reputation; many news-reporters had come here during the last few days.

Dilip returned to the car after obtaining directions.

They reached the house and found that two policemen were posted at the entrance.

He asked the policemen a few general questions about the case. Then, he requested them to show him the house from inside. They agreed to do so.

He wondered if he been there before? His memory was very hazy, and he could not recollect anything about this house.

He enquired from the policemen about Vijay Bahadur Singh who was mentioned in the newspaper reports as an absconder. "Can you tell me where this man lived"?

They said that his house was about ten minutes by car and gave directions to the chauffeur how to get there.

Soon, they reached Vijay Bahadur's house.

Sunny was quite sure that this was the house to which he had been brought on that fateful afternoon. He had a faint recollection of it as he had also visited it a few times with his parents.

He got down from the car and went towards the gate. There were two policemen standing there who stopped him and did not let him enter; perhaps they thought that he would tamper with evidence relating to the case.

Sunny asked, "Can I talk to any of the servants in the house"?

One of the policemen said, "We can let you do so only in our presence".

Sunny replied there was no problem with that.

Two servants were ushered by the policemen from inside the house. One was Bhola, the cook; the other was Basant, who did all the cleaning work there.

Sunny said, "I am trying to locate the sister of Vijay Bahadur Singh. Can you help me"?

Bhola, the older servant replied: "Vijay *Sahib* had only one sister named Radha who was married to a rich landlord named Shyam Singh Chaudhary from the nearby village of Chandrapur; however, she is not alive".

Sunny asked, "How far is Shyam Singh's house"?

Bhola replied, "It is not far from Surajpur. You can reach there in fifteen or twenty minutes depending on the traffic". He also gave the chauffeur some directions for reaching the place.

Sunny's excitement was now beyond description. His heart was beating faster than ever before.

Getting into the car, he urged the chauffeur "Quick! Take me to Chandrapur as fast as possible".

Sunny was thrilled that at long last, his search for his parents was coming to an end, and he was going to be re-united with them.

❑ ❑ ❑

It was only a short fifteen-minute drive to Chandrapur, but Sunny was impatient to get there. He told Dilip: "Why are you driving slowly? Faster!".

The chauffeur told him, "Please relax and be patient. The road is narrow, and I don't want to have an accident". He also asked: "What is the big hurry"?

What could Sunny tell him? Could he tell him that twenty-five years back, he had been kidnapped from that house, and that he could hardly wait to get there? Could he tell him that he was impatient to meet his parents after being separated from them for so long?

For Sunny, each passing minute was like an eon. The chauffeur could never have imagined the excitement of his passenger as the car made its way towards Chandrapur.

Soon, they reached a large, old house. The façade was covered with moss, and its boundary walls were crumbling. Dilip said that this was the address which they were looking for.

Sunny thought that he was mistaken, for it did not look like the house of his parents at all. He remembered it as a beautiful, white mansion. He also remembered that there used to be a big garden in front of that house where he used to run around and play, but he could not see any garden here. Instead, there was a big open space overgrown with wild shrubs and weeds where cattle were grazing.

He got down and asked a man standing nearby as to who lived in this house. The man replied that no one had lived here for many years except some servants who occupied the quarters at the back. Sunny asked him if he could speak to any of them; the man said he would go and see if anyone was around.

Soon, an old man appeared; he was walking with the help of a stick and came slowly towards them.

The chauffeur told the old man that his passenger was Mr. Sunny Thomas, a journalist who was writing a report about the serial child murders of Surajpur. He also said that they had just been to Surajpur, where they had visited the houses of both Mahinder Singh and Vijay Singh.

The old man greeted him and said, "My name is Nathu, and I used to be the cook in this house".

Sunny asked, "Can you help me with some details about Vijay Bahadur Singh"? "Did he often come to this house"?

Nathu replied: "He came here sometimes as his sister Radha was married to Shyam Singh Chaudhary". "Vijay Bahadur destroyed all happiness here", he added.

Sunny asked, "Why do you say so"?

Nathu replied, "Shyam Singh's elder brother Ram Singh Chaudhary had a son named Sonu who disappeared when he was not even four years old", and added, "I am sure that Vijay Bahadur Singh kidnapped him as no other person had come to the house that afternoon except him".

"What happened after that"? Sunny was very tense as he asked this question.

Nathu continued: "During the days following Sonu's disappearance, there was complete chaos and turmoil in this house. His mother Devika was totally shattered and did not touch any food at all for three days. Even after that, her husband and the servants had to force her to eat. Devika would think of all the terrible suffering that her little son could be undergoing. This would make her cry for hours on end. Sometimes she would sob gently, while at other times she would howl as loudly as she could. Her nerves were frayed, and she became completely withered within no time".

Nathu added: "No one was surprised when a few days later Devika had a nervous breakdown. She would be crying one moment, then laughing the next as she hallucinated that her Sonu was back with her".

"One day, she shouted excitedly that she had seen Sonu in the garden below and jumped from the balcony as if she was going to fly down towards him. She was dead as soon as she hit the ground".

"Ram Singh Chaudhary continued to make efforts to find his son. He met the Superintendent of Police several times but was informed that there was simply no trace of Sonu".

"His son's disappearance together with his wife's tragic demise had shattered him, and each passing day made him more depressed and withdrawn. A few weeks later he suffered a heart attack and died. After his death, the search for Sonu slowed down and then came to a halt. For all practical purposes, he was also presumed dead".

❑ ❑ ❑

Sunny felt a lump in his throat as he learnt about the tragedies that had befallen his parents.

He asked: "What happened to Ram Singh's younger brother who was married to Vijay Bahadur's sister? Where does he live"?

Nathu replied: "Shyam Singh, too had only one son named Raju who fell into bad company when he grew up and became an alcoholic. One evening, they were all going to Allahabad by car; Raju was quite drunk and should not have been driving the car. He crashed into a truck coming from the opposite direction, and all three of them—Raju as well as his parents-- died on the spot".

Nathu continued: "No one from this family has survived, and that is why no one lives in this house any more. Sharda Devi, the only sister of Ram Singh has lived in Patna since her marriage. She has inherited the estate. However, she does not come to this house as she considers it an ill-fated place which has brought such bad luck to everyone. Some people have even started saying that the place may be haunted. That is why this mansion, which was so grand and stately at one time, has become so forlorn and abandoned".

❑ ❑ ❑

Sunny had held it against Rosy that she had not sought the help of the police, who could have tried to restore him to his parents. However, he now realised that both his parents had died within a few weeks of his kidnapping-- well before Rosy had even met him.

He asked Nathu, "Can you show me the house from inside"?

Nathu was reluctant and said that the place would be full of dust and cobwebs as no one had lived there for years. However Sunny insisted, and Nathu agreed to do so. How could he have imagined that the house meant so much to the visitor!

Nathu first showed him the huge Drawing Room. Sunny could not remember anything about it; perhaps he had hardly been there as a child.

However, when Nathu showed him the Dining Room, he did recognize the big, oval shaped dining table where he used to sit between his parents when they had lunch or dinner.

He could also remember the verandah and the courtyard where he used to play a lot.

At his request, Nathu showed him the family rooms upstairs occupied by Ram Singh, Devika and Sonu, explaining that their decor had later been changed by Raju, who had lived there until his death in the car accident. For example, the pin-up posters on the walls had been put up by Raju, as also the bar in a corner of the room.

Throughout their conversation, Sunny had been careful not to disclose his real identity, nor why this house meant so much to him. He was trying to pose as a curious journalist, which is how Dilip had introduced him.

However, when he went to the balcony outside the bedroom, he remarked: "There used to be a big '*jhoola*' (swing) here". He could remember how he would often sit with his mother on the swing, looking at the garden below and enjoying the gentle breeze.

Nathu was a bit surprised and said: "Yes, you are absolutely correct. But how did you know"?

Sunny realized that he had made a slip, and he tried to evade the question.

However, Nathu was not a fool. He may have become withered with age, but the grey cells in his head were still going strong.

145

He thought to himself "How does he know that there was a '*jhoola*' on the balcony if he is coming here for the first time"?

Then, in a voice filled with curiosity and excitement, he again posed his question to the visitor: "How do you know that"?

Sunny did not answer the question. Instead he just pressed Nathu's hand and said: "It does not matter".

Sunny was aware that this man, who had served his family for many decades was now struggling to cope with old age. He asked him if he worked anywhere, and whether he had any income.

Nathu's voice choked with emotion. He said, "How can I work when I cannot even walk properly". Nathu added that his son supported him from his meagre earnings.

Sunny decided that henceforth he would take care of this old man who had served his parents. He gave him five hundred rupees and said: "I will look after your needs, but please don't discuss about my visit with anyone".

Nathu smiled and said, "I promise that I will not say anything to anyone, not even to my son". He felt such happiness as he had not felt in ages. He was sure that the visitor was none other than the long lost Sonu.

❑ ❑ ❑

Sunny asked: "Do you have any idea where Vijay Bahadur Singh could be hiding".

Nathu replied "No one knows where he is. If he is found, he will be lynched by the people. There are many persons in this area whose children had disappeared, and they are angry with him as he had a hand in all these crimes".

As Sunny began to leave the house and go towards the taxi, Nathu urged him, "Please visit the temple of Lord Shiva which Thakur Ram Singh had constructed in the village.

Sunny was a bit reluctant as he wanted to head back to Allahabad, but Nathu implored him and said that Shiva would bless him, adding, "If you go there, it will give happiness to Thakur Ram Singh's soul".

Sunny agreed to go to the temple. He asked Nathu to come with him as the chauffeur would not know the way.

The temple was at a short distance from the house. On the way, they passed by the village school. Its broken walls and dilapidated building were pointers to the utter neglect by the administration.

Nathu said: "Ram Singh's wife Devika remained childless for fifteen years after their marriage, and on the advice of his astrologer he built this temple to get Shiva's blessings. Then Sonu was born", whispering "I mean you were born".

As he spoke, he looked at Sunny with great affection, wondering what he would say. Sunny kept quiet and pretended that he had not heard the last bit.

The temple was very crowded. Devotees had come with flowers, money and sweets as offerings.

Nathu asked Sunny to touch the deity's feet and make an offering also.

Although Sunny did not believe in such rituals, he did not want to disappoint him and did as the latter had suggested. Moreover, he wanted to be respectful to the memory of his father, who had built the temple.

Sunny touched Shiva's feet, took out a hundred rupee note and placed it there as an offering.

The head priest was sitting on one side of the deity and singing *'bhajans'* (religious songs). Some other priests were sitting behind him and singing along with him; one of them was also playing the harmonium as he sang along. Sunny thought that they sang very well.

All the priests were wearing saffron-coloured clothes and had various kinds of garlands around their necks; some of them also had long hair and beards.

Nathu excitedly pulled him to one side. He said there was something very important which he wanted to tell him.

Sunny thought that maybe Nathu wanted him to give a bigger offering to the deity. He asked, "Should I offer more money as offering"?

Nathu was extremely excited and was pulling at his sleeve. Sunny wondered what the matter was.

Nathu whispered in his ear: "Look at all the temple priests. The man sitting all by himself in the last row is not really a priest. He is Vijay Bahadur Singh".

Sunny looked carefully at that man and asked: "Are you sure"?

Nathu said: "Absolutely sure". He added: "The beard and the long hair are both false. I am sure that his man is indeed Vijay".

Nathu was so sure that Sunny decided to trust him. He asked him to come outside.

They got into the taxi. Sunny told Dilip that he wanted to go to the Police Station. Nathu gave directions for getting there.

They were at the Police Station within a few minutes. Sunny took the Inspector aside and whispered to him: "Nathu has recognized Vijay Bahadur Singh who is absconding in the serial murders case. We can lead you to him".

The Inspector said, "Let's go". He immediately got into his jeep along with two constables, and they followed the taxi as it rushed back to the temple.

"Vijay Bahadur is inside", said Sonu.

The Inspector told the constables "Go from the front entrance while I will block the side door in case there is any attempt to escape through that".

Panicking as he saw the two constables approaching in his direction, Vijay got up and started to run towards the side door. While running, he pulled out a pistol and shot at one of the policemen, hitting him in the shoulder.

In the very next instant, the Inspector fired at him from the side door. Vijay was shot in the chest; he collapsed on the floor near the feet of Shiva's statue and died immediately.

The photograph showing Vijay lying in a pool of blood at the feet of Shiva's statue appeared in all the major newspapers the next day.

A legend would soon evolve how Lord Shiva had lured this demon into his temple and killed him there!

❑ ❑ ❑

Sunny was still shaken by the events which had taken place during the day.

He along with Nathu went back to the Police Station. Sunny wanted to ensure that Nathu should get the reward which the police had placed on Vijay Singh.

The day had turned out to be a mixed one for Sunny. On one hand, he had been devastated when he learnt about the tragic demise of his parents; on the other hand, he was happy that Vijay Bahadur Singh, a modern-day demon, had been killed.

It was late evening, and Sunny wanted to get back to his hotel in Allahabad. However, he had something more to accomplish.

He asked Nathu: "Can you give me the address of Ram Singh's sister Sharda?

Nathu replied "I do not have the address, but I can you give her telephone number".

Sunny took the phone number; he had a plan about how he should proceed.

He was now the real heir to whatever remained of his family's estate. However, he had gone missing twenty-five years back and had been presumed dead. He now had a new identity as Sunny Thomas, and he wanted things to continue this way.

At the same time wanted to restore his ancestral house while also helping the people here.

Next morning, he called up Sharda. She was his aunt, but he had no intention of disclosing his real identity to her. He merely told her, "I want to purchase your house in Chandrapur".

She herself had been keen to get rid of the house as it was of no use to her, and she replied that she was willing to sell it.

He asked, "Can you come over to Allahabad for finalizing the details"?

. She replied: "I will not be able to travel as I am unwell. However, I will send my son Ajay instead".

Sunny asked, "Can he come soon"?

He added, "I would like to leave Allahabad after our meeting".

It was agreed that Ajay would take the night train and be in Allahabad next morning.

❑ ❑ ❑

Ajay came to meet Sunny the next morning in the latter's hotel. Sunny wanted to give him an affectionate hug; after all, they were cousins.

However, he checked himself from doing any such thing. Instead, he just gave him a business-like hand shake.

During the meeting, Sunny agreed to purchase the house for two lakh rupees for the PEARLS group. Ajay was delighted that he got a good price for an abandoned and useless property. On the other hand, Sunny was thrilled at being able to buy the property; for him it was priceless.

He decided to use the building as a school for the village children. In this manner, he could prevent his ancestral home from further decay and ruin while also doing something which would benefit the people of Chandrapur.

It was arranged that Polly, who headed the Pearls group in India would contact Ajay and complete all the necessary formalities for making the payment and transferring the ownership of the building to the PEARLS group.

❑ ❑ ❑

His father had built a temple of Shiva for the village folk, and he was now going to set up a temple of learning—a school which would impart free education to their children.

None of the schools which the PEARLS Group had set up meant as much to Sunny as this school which he was now going to set up in Chandrapur. He looked up at the sky and smiled. He felt as if his parents were watching him from above, and that they too were smiling with pride.

✦ ✦ ✦

EPILOGUE

After returning to Dubai, Sunny continued to follow developments in the 'Surajpur Case'. One day, he read a report that Mahinder and Joginder had escaped from the jail in Surajpur. They had been caught by the villagers and lynched. He wondered whether they had really escaped, or whether the Police had allowed them to do so to let the villagers deal with them as they deemed appropriate.

Five more years passed by, during which period The PEARLS Group rapidly set up schools in several other countries.

However, Sunny was greatly tormented by the memories of his childhood.

Often, his mind travelled back to the months which he had spent at the 'ousbah' he was saddened at the fact that the pernicious practice of using child jockeys continued, and that it placed these small children in a terrible form of slavery, as he knew only too well from experience.

On 29th July, 2002, Sheikh Zayed, President of UAE and the Ruler of Abu Dhabi officially announced a ban on child camel jockeys, and Qatar followed suit in 2005. Both countries introduced robotic jockeys to replace children.

Sunny was happy at this development and hoped that the trend would become more widespread; he hoped that all Arab countries where camel racing takes place would completely ban the use of child jockeys.

However, Sunny remains concerned by reports that the evil practice continues. He is equally concerned that a child is reportedly kidnapped in India every eight minutes and that child trafficking remains rampant.

✦ ✦ ✦